THE BILLIONAIRE'S RIVAL

JEANNETTE WINTERS

Jeannette Winters
Author Contact

website:
JeannetteWinters.com
email:
authorjeannettewinters@gmail.com
Facebook:
Author Jeannette Winters
Twitter:
JWintersAuthor
Newsletter Signup:
www.jeannettewinters.com/newsletter

Also follow me on:
BookBub:
bookbub.com/authors/jeannette-winters
Goodreads:
https://www.goodreads.com/author/show/
13514560.Jeannette_Winters
Pinterest:
https://www.pinterest.com/authorjw/boards/

THE BILLIONAIRE'S RIVAL

Charles Lawson carries the weight of the entire family's future on his shoulders. As CEO of Lawson Steel it is his responsibility to ensure their legacy continued for the next generation. First on his agenda is to clean up loose ends from the past. Doing so is risky and if he fails, the price could be great. It's a risk he's willing to take.

Rosslyn Clark loves her life as is, but family is everything to her. When her parents find themselves in a crisis, all she loves is at risk. Whether she likes it or not, sometimes change is inevitable.

As Charles prepares to seal the deal, he finds one beautiful blonde stands in his way, and things become complicated. Can he continue with his original plan and look at her as collateral damage or has Rosslyn become something more to him?

Rosslyn finds herself caught between two powerful men, one she works for, the other, his rival. Will she do what is expected of her, or will she walk away from everything and follow her heart?

Charles Lawson leaned back in his high leather chair and glared at his brother Dylan. "There is more at risk than just that contract."

Dylan shook his head. "The only thing that matters is getting that contract signed. We'll deal with whatever issues come up later."

That's not going to happen. Charles could appreciate his brother's eagerness to get the next project off the ground, but his gut told him to let this one go. "We don't need it, Dylan."

"Need it, no. But I want this one," Dylan snarled.

Dylan was acting as though this was only going to affect him. That wasn't the case. "This isn't about you. It's about Lawson Steel. And although I value your opinion, I—"

"You don't want it."

Charles knew Dylan was out to prove himself, but as head of the company, it was Charles's responsibility to ensure they didn't get tangled up in anything that might tarnish the Lawson name. Dylan saw only one thing: the dollar amount on the bottom line. But they didn't need the money, none of them did. Which was why he didn't jump at this opportunity.

His experience had shown him that anyone willing to overpay to get what they wanted usually had ulterior motives. Never had they been good ones either.

He wasn't willing to say they were unscrupulous people, but Charles didn't want their name linked to anything potentially . . . illegal. He didn't have any proof, but his gut was telling him to walk away from this one. Sometimes your gut was all you had to go on.

"I listen to your opinion no differently than others. But I need you to trust me on this. Something's not right."

Frustration was written all over Dylan's face as he responded, "I looked over the contract myself. It's clean. Hell, I've never seen one so detailed without errors."

Exactly. Charles heard over and over again how perfect this deal was. He'd learned many years earlier nothing was perfect. You could only hope the flaws weren't numerous or serious. *And if you don't rush, you can limit the negative exposure.*

Dylan headed to the door but turned back and snapped, "You're really not going to budge on this are you?"

It was a stance he was forced to take, even if it meant putting a bigger wedge between him and Dylan. "Until I feel comfortable that it is not going to blow up in our face, consider this deal off the table."

Dylan slammed the door behind him as he left the office. *That went fucking well.* As a whole, the family had always been close growing up. Dylan was the baby of the family and hadn't been ready for their father to retire and the next generation to step up. But Dylan seemed to harbor more resentment toward Charles than the others. Of course it didn't help when Charles told Dylan that he wasn't ready for such responsibility.

He needed to get over it. That comment had been a few

years ago when Dylan had just finished college. At that time, Dylan was like every young man in his mid-twenties . . . invincible, or at least they believe they are. Charles had seen too many of his friends make mistakes; some didn't live long enough to regret those mistakes. It wasn't something he had wanted for Dylan or any of his brothers. As the eldest, it was his job to keep them in line, even if that meant they hated him for it.

Of course Dylan didn't prove Charles wrong. If anything he showed Charles just what a fuck-up he could be. Dylan never got arrested, but for a few years he lived his life on the edge and very much in the public eye. Dylan squandered the family's money on fast cars and even faster women. For a short time, Dylan had his face plastered all over the tabloids. More than once Charles thought for sure Dylan was going to be the one to tarnish the Lawson name. Thankfully that phase seemed to have passed. Now he needed to deal with Dylan challenging every decision Charles made.

Lawson men were thickheaded. It was a family trait. Being told no, or you were wrong, wasn't easy for any of them to swallow. And with age, it seemed to be getting worse, at least for Charles.

Dylan said it was because Charles was more like their grandfather than any of them. He hoped that wasn't the case. Since Charles was the one who'd spent so much time with their father, he was unlucky enough to have spent the most time with their grandfather as well. That's why he knew just how screwed-up their grandfather actually had been. The guy had some serious issues. Control freak was nothing compared to his verbal abuse. It wasn't bestowed upon Charles or any of his siblings, but he'd seen plenty of it upon their father. Charles couldn't believe some of the shit he'd heard. There were a few times he thought for sure they'd come to blows, but they never did. His father, although a tough son of a bitch, never retaliated. Charles wasn't so sure he could've held back if it had been him.

He'd asked his father about it once, why he didn't knock his grandfather on his ass and end it. His father said it was his job to end the cycle. Although Charles tried asking what that meant, his father never spoke of it again. Hopefully that behavior had ended with their grandfather because Charles couldn't imagine anyone, let alone a child, being treated like . . . *a total worthless piece of shit.*

Because of what he'd witnessed, Charles was careful to watch his temper and tried to choose his words wisely. He never wanted to be like their grandfather. But Dylan knew exactly how to provoke him, like he wanted Charles to lose control. *Maybe he wants me to fail. To show me I'm not the right person for the job just like I did to him.*

He wouldn't ever admit that had crossed his mind a few times. But second guessing his father's decision wasn't going to do any good. At that moment, all he could do was stay focused and do what was expected of him. The price he paid for being the eldest.

Charles picked up the contract Dylan had left in his office. He wished there was something concrete to go on. He knew Dylan was going to let the others know what a stubborn ass Charles was being over this. It was only a matter of time before one of them, if not all, started to show up at the office, trying to make peace between the two.

However that wasn't a quarrel between his brothers he could just let go. This was business and no one was going to make him change his mind, no matter how much they pleaded. *Hate me if you must Dylan, but I know I'm right.*

Charles didn't have the time or energy to seek concrete proof just to appease his brother. The company didn't need the money or the contract. It was a moot point, and he wasn't wasting resources on something that wasn't going to happen.

Tossing the contract back on his desk, he returned to what he should be focusing on. There was a new project coming up in Dubai that needed all the specifications reviewed for the final time before signing off on it. He'd been up half the night and all he needed was a few more hours and it would be set to go. As long as no unforeseen issues arose in the meantime.

Charles believed in triple checking. He'd created the initial drafts, but they went through a lot of hands afterward. It was his job to ensure any changes didn't affect the building's integrity. Moving an electrical outlet was one thing, but certain things were non-negotiable. Every once in a while a client asked for the impossible and some on Charles's staff weren't able to say no. *I have no problem being the bad guy.* It was his name on the line after all.

He was almost finished when his cell phone rang. Their father was the only person Charles knew Dylan wouldn't grumble to. So which brother was it going to be? *Gareth?* He and Dylan were more alike than they'd want to admit. No way Dylan had sought his assistance. Hell, if anything, Dylan was more likely to complain about Gareth not pulling his weight. Gareth was the brother who rarely wanted anything to do with the company. But Charles wasn't letting him off the hook, even if it meant having him do some unconventional, and probably unnecessary, research.

"Hello Gareth. That didn't take long?"

"I'm efficient."

There was no doubt Gareth had looked over everything thoroughly. Charles also knew his motivation was to get it done and over with. Gareth was useful to the company with his knack of finding things no one else could. He was almost tempted to let him dig into that contract Dylan brought him.

But doing so would open a door Charles already considered closed.

"Is there anything I should know?" Charles asked.

"You want to meet for lunch and discuss what I found?"

That wasn't an answer. "Why don't you come to my office now? I'm free at the moment."

There was no way Gareth hadn't heard him. "There is this cute waitress that—"

"I'm busy."

"I thought you said you were free," Gareth said.

Not to hear about your latest conquest. "To talk business."

"Charles, you need to loosen up a bit. It doesn't all fall on your shoulders, you know. We're all here to support you anytime you need it."

Charles bit back his sarcastic remark. Pissing off one brother a day was his limit. There had been a few occasions where he may have exceeded it. It was easy for Gareth and the others to say they were all in, but actually following through was another thing. Not only did they each have their own lives and businesses to maintain, they were still getting used to the day to day workings of Lawson Steel. It was going to take time to know when something was wrong.

Even though he didn't have time to screw off, this was his brother. Charles needed to make the time. If he didn't, the days turned into weeks and then into months before they saw each other socially. But he wasn't going out for "legs and eggs" as Gareth called it. Why exotic dance clubs served breakfast all day made as little sense as why his brother went there to eat.

"Lunch, at The Choice. I'll meet you in the lobby at one." Charles ended the call before Gareth could protest. Gareth probably wasn't actually in the building anyway. *This might be the only way to get him into the office.* Keeping him at a desk was going to take a lot more than anything Charles could come up with for him to do. *I probably would need to hire him a hot looking secretary. But then I'd have to deal with the sexual harassment complaints.* This was one of the days he wished he wasn't the CEO.

There might be six of them, but Charles was the one who'd worked by their father's side all along. It was a burden the others didn't understand, and truthfully, he didn't want them to. Since birth, Charles had been groomed for this. When the others were off spending their summers doing what they wanted, he was stuck going with his father from one construction site to another. The worst had been sitting quietly during the meetings. His father told him you learn a lot just watching people. Actions told more than words.

It probably was the most valuable lesson he'd learned, and he applied it to all his dealings. People thought he was quiet, and some accused him of being standoffish. They were way off the mark. He let them talk themselves into a corner and enjoyed watching as they tried to get themselves out.

This tactic had backfired a few times, usually when dealing with the opposite sex. He would listen, and then the moment came when they asked what he thought. Charles always gave them his honest opinion. It wasn't always accepted as well as he anticipated. Hell, a few times it made Dylan's reaction seem warm and friendly. He'd even caught a few slaps across the face, probably well-deserved in their eyes. But Charles was known for being brutally honest and had no time for idle chatter. Charles was all about Lawson Steel, all the time.

That wasn't the case for his siblings. They each had chosen their own paths, for the most part. But they had been groomed to someday work as a whole to take C. J. Lawson

Steel to the next level. What none of them knew, and couldn't, was a stipulation for Charles to continue running the company. Charles needed to somehow unite them but not by having them all work in the same building.

There was one contract Lawson Steel had never been able to obtain. Not only did he need to knock Grayson, their only competitor he took seriously, out of the running, but he also needed all five of his brothers to agree to sign the contract. Since they were butting heads on the insignificant ones, he was dreading what was going to happen when he broached the subject. From how his meeting with Dylan had gone, he might be creating a bigger wedge instead of making progress.

Charles didn't intentionally piss Dylan off, but he wasn't going to give in when he knew he was right either. Charles had been taught how to manage anyone, but family was different, and he needed to somehow learn a new way. This was something he couldn't ask his father for advice on either.

This business had been passed down for several generations. Hell, Charles was the seventh generation of Lawsons to man the helm. He was proud of the legacy, no different than being named after them all. Charles Joseph Lawson the Seventh. The title came with power and prestige in the business world.

The only drawback from that title was the endless pressure to ensure someday there was an eighth in line to carry on the name. Charles was in no rush to tie the knot. He was thirty-eight, not ninety-eight. There was plenty of time to have children, if he wanted.

That was the key, if *he* wanted. No matter what his father thought, Charles wasn't marrying to provide an heir. And the way things were going, it didn't look like he'd be marrying for love either. He was willing to take on the company, and all the responsibility that went along with it. But no one was pushing him into anything more than that. His personal life was off limits. His brothers had gotten that message a long time ago, their father, not so much.

But times were changing faster than his father could keep up with or understand. This generation was global. It was nothing for him to be in New York one week then Dubai the next for work with a stop in Paris to meet friends for dinner. The need to be on each job site in person, ensuring everything was as designed, no longer was required. People were hired to video and photograph every step of the construction. Not just per the contract, but for insurance purposes as well. It was all about covering your ass, or assets as Charles called it.

When his father ran the business, if a customer had an issue, you talked it out like men, sometimes shouting a few threats, but that was all, and then you fixed whatever the customer thought was wrong. Now everything was done through a third party. The only time you found out there was a problem was when you heard about it from a lawyer, and it was settled in court if not negotiated prior to that. There were definitely people who used the court system to make money. But those should be held accountable, because they chose to use substandard materials, and that was something Charles never would tolerate.

Things like that made Charles very particular about which contact he was signing. No matter what Dylan believed, once a contractor was questioned for unethical behaviors, guilty or not, he proceeded with twice as much caution. *A leopard doesn't change its spots. It just learns to hunt more wisely.* And Charles needed to be a tad smarter than them, so he didn't fall for anyone's bullshit.

The grandfather clock chimed once. The morning had gotten away from him with distractions that were . . . unnecessary. *And that's exactly what this lunch with Gareth is.*

. . .

Rosslyn Clark was running late. If she kept her uncle waiting any longer, he was going to complain to her father. *If he hadn't already.* But the job hadn't been her idea, and the way her morning had gone, the universe was telling her not to take it.

Rosslyn needed to work, and her uncle was willing to bring her in with a salary she could only dream of. How she could actually earn that amount was beyond her. Rosslyn had told her father it was out of her comfort zone. She was great with people and would make a great receptionist, but what did she know about being a personal assistant?

Rosslyn told herself it was going to be like scheduling her own day's activities, just with a bigger expense account and a lot more at stake. Outside of scheduling things, Rosslyn had no idea what a personal assistant did. *Probably pick up dry cleaning and bring him coffee. Two things I know I can do.*

As she entered the restaurant she was greeted by the hostess. "Welcome to The Choice. Do you have a reservation?"

Rosslyn didn't miss the once-over the hostess gave her. *You're no different than me. We both get paid by the hour.* Holding her tongue, she forced a smile and said, "I'm meeting Unc—Mr. Maxwell Grayson."

The hostess nodded and said, "Please follow me."

This was a five-star restaurant, and Rosslyn didn't frequent them often. On occasion she attended a dinner with her father to meet with her uncle, but she found places like this too . . . stiff. She always worried about spilling something on her blouse or using the wrong fork. She didn't grow up in a house where she needed to worry about such things.

Rosslyn couldn't believe her mother was Uncle Max's sister. They were so . . . different. There was only one word she could use to describe him. *Cold.* She wasn't sure if it was out of fear of losing his fortune, but when her mother ran away and eloped, marrying the family limo driver, she had been cut off from the entire family. At least financially. They were always invited to family functions. Most of which they didn't attend. *Like we could afford the tux for Dad, never mind gowns for Mom and me.*

She wouldn't be here now if she wasn't desperate for a job. She hated being in the city. Living in upstate New York had its perks. Like a yard and a lot less traffic. The downside was there wasn't much work available. At least not the type she wanted. And they needed money.

Her mother's medical bills were mounting and neither of her parents were willing to accept money from Uncle Max. As far as Rosslyn knew, Max didn't even know how sick her mother was. That was sad. Her mother would rather suffer in pain than take a penny from her family.

And here I am about to work for him.

At least she hadn't lied to her parents as to what she was doing or why. There may have been one thing she'd left out. How much she hated it. But she loved her mother, and if this was what she needed to do in order to pay the bills, then so be it. They'd given her the best life they could, and now it was her turn to carry the weight for a while.

When she arrived at the table she could tell her uncle was upset about her tardiness. What Rosslyn excelled at was winning people over with her positive attitude. *Smile and the world smiles with you.* She wasn't sure that worked on people who appeared to have more money than God. It was worth a try. With all she could muster, she smiled, walked around the table, and kissed him on the cheek. "Uncle Max, it seems like forever since I've seen you."

He didn't return the warm greeting. "If you missed me so much, I'd have thought you'd be early."

Some things never change. She wasn't going to grovel for a job or kiss his ass either. But she was willing to ignore some unpleasant remarks for her mother's sake. Swallowing her pride she said, "I'm sorry I kept you waiting." She took the seat opposite him. Normally with family or friends, she opted to sit closer. But then again, she wasn't worried they'd bite her head off either.

"I'm sure it won't happen again. Not if you want this job."

"No sir, it won't." She'd give her best as she would to any employer.

"Good. I spoke to human resources and they are expecting you to arrive tomorrow at eight."

"I'll be there . . . on time."

"Aunt Laura is in Paris doing some shopping. I have an event tonight. I'd like it if you would attend with me. I can have a car come and collect you at eight."

Spending money was all Aunt Laura seemed good at. At least that's what she'd overheard her parents saying a few times over the years. Apparently, nothing had changed. Rosslyn definitely couldn't be a stand-in for Laura. Laura was . . . elegant and graceful. Rosslyn couldn't wear heels higher than three inches because she was afraid she'd stumble. How was she going to bow out when it didn't sound like an invite as much as an order?

"Uncle Max—"

"If you're going to work for me, I'd prefer if people didn't know we were related. It might cause some unwanted friction amongst the staff."

She was totally fine with that. "Should I call you Mr. Grayson?"

He nodded. "But when we're alone, Maxwell will be fine."

Oh this is going to be fun. She'd never had to address any of her former employers so formally. Was he this way with all his employees or was she just the lucky one? *Making me pay for asking for help? Wouldn't surprise me.* But all that mattered to her right now was a paycheck each week.

"I didn't bring anything appropriate for a black tie event," Rosslyn stated, knowing damn well she didn't have anything back home either. The only thing she had even close to fancy was a white maxi dress that hugged her breasts and flowed loosely everywhere else.

"I thought every woman had a little black dress in their closet."

Rosslyn chuckled. "Black really isn't my color."

In the same flat tone Max said, "Tonight it is." He reached into his pocket and pulled out his wallet. Then he slid five one-hundred dollar bills across the table to her. "This should be enough." He got up from his seat and said, "Remember, the driver will be there at eight o'clock sharp."

Rosslyn nodded, and he left. *Mom is doing better. Thanks for asking, Uncle Max. It's good to see that you care.*

Slipping the money into her purse, Rosslyn got up from her seat and started to walk out of the restaurant without having a glass of water, never mind eating. Out of the corner of her eye she saw two men sitting at a table off to one side. Was it her imagination or were they staring at her? For the briefest second, she made eye contact with one of them. His dark eyes seemed to peer right through her.

Rosslyn had no clue who either of them were, but if they'd seen Uncle Max slip her the money, it was no wonder they were looking at her like that. It wasn't uncommon for such practices to take place, even in nice establishment like this. *Who cares what they think? At least they'll assume I'm a well-paid call girl.*

She could set them straight, but why? It didn't matter. The odds of seeing either of them again in this city was highly unlikely. She doubted they ordered off a dollar menu or enjoyed a coffee for a buck. She was out of her class in this place, but at least she could exit with some dignity.

Holding her head up proudly, she left the building. Once outside, she was faced with the loud noise of the city. Rosslyn had no idea which way to head, so she hailed a taxi. She hoped they would take her to the right place. As she stood on the curbside waiting, she knew this was just the beginning of what she suspected would be a very odd day. First stop, a dress shop. Then back to the hotel and hope she could make herself . . . presentable.

Who was she kidding? A dress was one thing, but her hair was a wild mess. Rosslyn had no idea who she'd be meeting with tonight and needed to ensure she didn't embarrass Uncle —Mr. Grayson.

She really should've had her hair cut before she came to the city. It would've been so much more cost effective, because she would've had one of her friends do it. Now she needed to find a salon that would take a walk-in and wouldn't charge an arm and a leg for it.

Rosslyn hated to admit it, but she needed to make the five hundred dollars go a lot further than a dress.

When the taxi driver pulled up to the curb, she got inside and said, "Can you take me to the most reasonable consignment shop around? I have a party to go to."

The driver nodded. "My brother owns one just out of the city. It'll cost you seventy-five bucks for me to take you there and back."

"Fancy dresses?" she asked.

What she'd save on the dress would definitely be worth it. "Does he cut hair too?"

The driver chuckled. "Are you looking for a buzz cut?" Her eyes widened and she shook her head. "Then I suggest a place not far from my brother's shop."

It wasn't going to make much sense to have the driver wait for her the entire time. "Maybe you can give me your number and I'll call you when I'm finished? I need to be back in the city early."

"I'll visit my family while waiting."

"Are you sure?"

"Yes. If I don't spend time with my nephews and my niece at least once a week, they call me crying, saying they miss me."

Rosslyn had no idea what that was like. Her uncle hadn't seemed to give a crap about her as a child. Even now, there was no warmth in his eyes when he looked at her. If anything, it almost looked like he resented that she . . . existed.

I guess the only thing Uncle Max loves is his money.

2

Rosslyn's heart was pounding so hard she was sure it could be seen through this dress. But she was here and even if she had to say it herself, she looked pretty damn good.

She'd taken a selfie before the limo arrived. Her friends back home weren't going to believe it. It'd been a long time since she'd worn her hair above her shoulders. For years it had been so long that when she wore it in a braid down the middle of her back, it almost touched her butt. At least cutting off thirteen inches hadn't been for nothing. The hair stylist said it would be donated to make wigs for cancer patients. That's all it took to turn her entire day around.

Doing something for someone else always made her feel better. She wished she had enough money that her job could be volunteering to help the needy. Rosslyn wasn't bitter, but she couldn't understand how a brother and sister could be so different. Her mother would've given away her last penny if there was someone who needed it more. Maxwell had more money than one could spend in a lifetime, and everything he gave was based on one thing only, how it made him look to the world.

Rosslyn had no idea what the event was, but she was positive *Mr. Grayson* was there to be noticed. If she was expected to be by his side, she was going to be thrown into the center of attention as well. There was no way they would be able to hide that they were related for very long. The media was better than hiring a private investigator. They could find skeletons in your closet that you didn't even know you had. *I bet Uncle Max has quite a few. Probably pays them to keep their mouths shut.*

She made her way through the sea of luxuriously dressed individuals. The good thing about shopping at a consignment shop, no one was wearing the same dress she was. It was so last year, or even older. Rosslyn only saw two things: it fit her shape and her wallet. Was it wrong that she had extra cash and no plans to offer it back to her uncle? She considered it payment for her time tonight. And besides, it wasn't like the money was going to something foolish. It was going to the medical bills. *If he knew that, he'd probably demand it back.*

She didn't like living like that. Back home things were much more open and honest. She was free to be herself. Now she needed to be who Uncle Max expected her to be. Of course she wasn't sure what that was. But she was going to find out.

Her uncle spotted her from across the room. With a tilt of his head, she knew he wanted her to join him. On the way she snagged a glass of champagne. She wasn't fond of the stuff, but it gave her something to do with her hands instead of fidgeting.

There was a hesitation about what she was supposed to call him. Mr. Grayson? Maxwell? She waited for him to address her.

"Rosslyn, this is Mary Lou. Her son will be doing an internship with us."

Mary Lou was beaming with pride. "Mr. Grayson, I can't thank you enough. I'd been praying that either you or Lawson Steel would accept him."

She saw her uncle's jaw twitch, but he said nothing. Rosslyn probably should've done some research on who was who in the business, but she didn't think she'd be in a situation where it was needed. Smiling she said, "He's made the right choice."

Max turned to her and for a moment appeared to give his approval. It was short-lived. "If you'll excuse us, we have several other parents who are equally eager to discuss their child's future."

"Of course. Thank you again, Mr. Grayson. I'm sure you'll be impressed," Mary Lou said.

As they left Mary Lou standing there, Max said, "Every parent thinks their child is a genius. Most are bloody idiots."

Rosslyn thought about how many times her parents had bragged about her abilities. *I'm sure I will be an utter disappointment to you as well, Uncle Max.* Hoping to get an understanding as to why she was there, Rosslyn asked, "Is there something you require me to do tonight?"

He replied, "Yes. Do you see the man talking to the woman with the red dress on?"

Rosslyn scanned the room and only saw one person wearing red. The man beside her almost looked like the man she'd seen earlier at the restaurant. It was hard to tell because everyone looked different in a tux. "I do."

"Good. I want you to keep track of each person he speaks to. And by the end of the night, I want to make sure we have spoken to every single one as well. But mind you, only *after* he has talked to them. Understood?"

It seemed very straight forward. "Yes."

"And whatever you do, stay the hell away from him," Max snarled.

Whoever he was, her uncle obviously didn't like him. Of course, that didn't mean anything. Max wasn't what one would call a very likable guy. She spent the rest of the evening doing exactly as Max had instructed. And it wasn't long before she realized that the other man represented Lawson Steel. Evidently, that was her uncle's rival. What she found humorous was Max made it sound as though Lawson Steel was insignificant. But his actions said otherwise.

Was the man actually *the Mr. Lawson*? Rosslyn watched him closely; he carried himself as though he could be. At times he had the same look her uncle had. One that wished he was anywhere but there. It seemed to be prevalent among the guests. Except for the parents pimping out their children's talents, no one seemed happy to be in attendance. Not even her.

"Do you need transportation home?" Max asked.

She had expected him to provide it both ways, but once again, she shouldn't have assumed. "I'm all set."

"Good. Don't forget, eight a.m."

"I'll be there." *Tired but I'll be there.*

She hadn't planned on a late night right before her first day on the job. Rosslyn still didn't know how any of this played into being a personal assistant. She could only imagine what tomorrow would bring. Hopefully something in the office, where she could be off her feet. One thing about being in the city, you did a lot more walking than driving. Mostly because you could walk faster than the traffic seemed to move. There was nothing pleasant about that when wearing heels. She should've gotten the hint when she saw women dressed in business attire and wearing sneakers.

There was no way she could walk to the hotel even if she

19

had the energy to do so. If it wasn't so late, she'd have texted that nice taxi driver from earlier. He did say to do so at any time, but it was past midnight. It would be rude and asking too much.

The chatter from the other guests made it impossible for her to think clearly. Stepping onto the balcony, she pulled out her phone and searched for taxis in her area. As she went through the list, she had a feeling she was being watched. Turning around, she saw the one man she wasn't supposed to interact with. His tie was loosened and his shirt was partially unbuttoned. Had he already been on the balcony when she came out? She'd been dying for some fresh air and hadn't noticed.

"I believe your . . . date has left," he said.

Sticking with her instructions, she replied simply, "I'm more than capable of finding my own way home, thank you."

The way he looked at her made her shudder. "I'm sure you are. I was just leaving, and if you'd like—"

"No thank you," she said firmly. Max said don't talk to him. She was positive he'd flip if she accepted a ride. "I already told you, I can find my *own* way home."

He cocked a brow and said, "You've made that clear. I was going to ask if you wanted to have a drink with me, we could discuss your opinion on how the event went."

She didn't know him and didn't want to either. There was no way he cared what her thoughts were one way or another. The closer he got, she was positive he was the same man from the restaurant. Did he recognize her as well? She did have a transformation since this morning.

"I really don't have an opinion." She hoped that was enough to drop the subject. His comment almost blew her away.

"Even someone like you has an opinion."

Like me? It was like a slap in the face. *Breathe, Rosslyn. Don't make a scene. He's not worth it. Think of Mom.* She had a lot to say, but opted to go a different way. "I think Maxwell would be a better person to ask. Now if you'll excuse me," Rosslyn said and tried to slip past him.

Her spiked heel caught between two boards on the balcony, causing her to stumble. She wobbled a bit but regained her balance. Unfortunately, not without hearing the snap. Looking down she saw the heel wedged in the decking and no longer attached to her shoe.

Rosslyn bent down and tried to pull the heel out. The thing wouldn't budge. "Let me," he said and brushed her hand away.

It would be ridiculous to deny his help. She needed to walk through a crowd of people to leave the building. She definitely would draw attention walking like this. While he pulled the heel out, she decided to take the other shoe off. It felt wonderful to have her toes free. Slipping off the broken one, she picked it up.

"I'm not sure I can fix this," he said, holding the heel up.

That was what she got for buying from the clearance rack. Taking the heel from him, she replied, "I have another pair."

"Most people do," he said. With her shoes in hand, she headed again for the doors leading inside. "There's another way."

"Excuse me?" she turned.

"There is a staircase around the corner. It leads directly to the parking lot."

Rosslyn walked over and looked over the railing. She could see the parking lot, but the pathway leading to it was poorly lit. "I might break more than my heel going that way."

"I'll carry you if you're worried about hurting your feet."

Rosslyn's feet couldn't hurt much more. "I wouldn't

accept a ride from you, what makes you think I'll allow you to carry me?"

"I don't assume anything. It was strictly an offer. Take it or leave it. I really don't care."

Rosslyn looked over the rocky pathway. He stood directly behind her, so close she could smell his cologne. *He smells as sexy as he looks.* Which provided her answer. No way was she getting in his arms for any reason. *Not even if the building was on fire.*

"Then you won't be offended when I decline your offer." She gripped her shoes tightly as she entered the building. She was wiped out both physically and emotionally. Right now she didn't care if the room erupted in laughter. To her knowledge, no one seemed to notice. The music was playing and the remaining people seemed to be enjoying the party, some a bit too much.

And now I know why Max left. The only ones who stayed obviously didn't need to work in the morning.

When she got outside, she asked the doorman if he could call a taxi for her. "We offer free transportation for those who feel it is best not to be behind a wheel."

She wasn't drunk, but then again, there she was standing outside holding her shoes. If it got her a ride home, let him think what he wanted. Smiling she said, "I'd appreciate that, thank you."

It wasn't long before she was on her way and could call it a night. She was tempted to call her friend Cassie to let her know how everything had gone. There might be a few things she'd need to keep to herself. *Like Mr. Lawson Steel.* If she even hinted about talking to someone that sexy, Cassie would keep her up all night, giving her the third degree. Sadly or thankfully, there wasn't really anything to say.

And it needs to stay that way. She wasn't blowing this job by not being able to resist one stinking man.

At least I know one place he won't be tomorrow. Grayson Corp.

Charles had been upset when his brother Seth backed out of attending the reception and he had to step in. Charles didn't buy the last minute excuse of having a stomach bug. He knew Dylan had spoken to Seth. This was their way of taking sides.

He should've seen it coming. Seth was always riding Charles's ass for being so tough on Dylan. What Seth didn't get was Charles was tough on everyone. Dylan wasn't singled out. The difference was Dylan pushed back more than the others.

He understood why. Dylan wanted to run Lawson Steel. Charles figured one day he probably would. The guy had some brilliant ideas. What he lacked was patience and how to play the game. It was like poker. If they know you have shit for cards, you lose. But keep them guessing, let them win a few, and only then when the stakes are high, do you go all in and take it all.

That's exactly what he was doing tonight with Grayson. Charles knew Maxwell had been monitoring him so he made sure he spoke to people who meant nothing to him. He'd already met with Gareth earlier and knew exactly who he wanted as his interns and the deal was already on the table.

Not showing tonight and playing the game would've tipped his hand. By the time Maxwell figured it out, Charles would've snagged the top candidates right out from under him. A small victory, but sweet, nonetheless.

And that's what happens, Maxwell, when you're all caught up in beautiful women instead of your business.

Charles had to admit, he would've been equally off his game if she'd accompanied him. Difference was he wouldn't have gone home alone. What was the point of Maxwell giving her a makeover and then shutting it down? *At least the money he slipped you hadn't been wasted. She looked...amazing.* Not that he wanted to admit he noticed. But it was hard not to. Hell, it was hard not to have noticed her when he saw her the first time in the restaurant.

Was it possible she was one of those ladies for hire who was eye candy only and nothing more? It would explain her refusal for him to give her a lift.

There were several high-priced call girls, but they were well known. This woman wasn't one of the regulars. *Where did you find her, Maxwell?*

As if Charles would ever consider hiring someone for the night. If he wanted a date, all he needed to do was pick up the phone. There were plenty of women who wanted his attention. Of course, he wasn't interested in giving them any.

So why did this woman catch his eye? What was different about her? It wasn't because she'd been with Maxwell. Unfortunately the guy was a piece a shit and not only in business. It was well known he ran around on his wife. The Grayson family might be his competition, but only because they didn't play by the rules. What they couldn't get, they bought. *And I can't imagine you having that woman any other way.*

Why did he care? The only time he and Maxwell bumped into each other was at those types of events. They were expected to show up to give a speech and encourage the youth that hard work and perseverance could make your dreams come true. He'd given the talk so many times even he didn't believe it any longer. What no one ever mentioned was the word luck.

Luck was a key component in the equation. Charles wasn't stupid. He knew he was lucky to have been born into his legacy. If not, would he be where he was now? Absolutely not. Hell, he wasn't sure if he would've been interested in building the tallest buildings in the world.

Everyone knew the penthouse was the place to be in a building. And that's where he lived. But he'd like a place to hide away. Something small. A neighborhood where people actually talked and cared about each other.

Sure he knew people in his building, but they were all superficial. He knew their dogs' names more than he did their children's names.

Yes, that was the life he was born to live. He couldn't help but wonder if she was born into that lifestyle as well. Charles couldn't picture a girl growing up and hoping one day she could become an escort. Someone with her looks should be a model.

Charles could never be with one of those either. Models loved the spotlight, and he hated it. No one really cared how you were doing, just what would sell. Since his life was strictly business, the tabloids left him alone. As his brothers told him on many occasions, he was too boring to make news. That was a good thing. Who the hell wanted strangers following them around snapping pictures and assuming they knew shit.

Although Charles did want to make the news, and hopefully it wouldn't take long. Things were falling into place. He just needed to stay focused and not let anything fuck it up.

Hell, maybe I should've asked for her number. I could've hired her to distract Maxwell more often. He laughed to himself and wondered if Gareth knew who she was. He hadn't said anything when they first saw her at The Choice.

That was unlike Gareth. Usually he was the one with the snappy remarks.

It didn't matter. Charles didn't need her help to bring Maxwell to his knees. He had his brothers to help accomplish that. When they were done with Grayson Corp, Maxwell would be lucky if he could get a job cleaning the buildings, never mind building them.

This rivalry had been going on long before Charles had taken over. It started when his father ran the company. A contract had been signed and approved. They were in the process of building when the inspectors showed up and found inadequate materials being used. It was only on one part of the building, a part his father swore they hadn't started working on. Everything about it looked like Lawson Steel had been set up.

The contract had been canceled and a new one had been signed with Grayson Corp. It was all too convenient. Maxwell had just taken over leadership of the company and obviously was willing to do anything to make a name for himself. As far as Charles was concerned, that name was asshole, and even then, that was being nice.

Charles was fortunate. He might have taken over as CEO, but he hadn't been thrown in like Maxwell. Grayson Corp was run and controlled by the eldest son. When he died, it all passed to his oldest son. That eliminated any need to compete among the siblings, but it also made a very select few power hungry.

Maxwell wielded a lot of power in New York City and around the world as well. Charles could easily have fought fire with fire, but he wasn't willing to stoop to his level. His father had been frank with him when he took over. He told him to think like an architect. You build them strong to last forever, but place explosives properly and it will implode onto itself.

That's exactly what Charles had planned. Not actually explosives, but let Maxwell's questionable dealings appear all at once. He'd be spinning, trying to figure out which one to cover up first, and his empire would unravel right before his eyes.

The only reason Lawson Steel stayed in business after that one incident was an impeccable reputation. Charles, with Gareth's help, had compiled so much shit on Maxwell the Feds might be interested in reviewing the file.

I just wish it was my father who was delivering the blow. But better late than never.

Since Maxwell didn't have any children and his marriage was a joke, there was nothing to hold Charles back from moving forward on this.

Once Maxwell was out of the picture, Lawson Steel would be back on top, where it belonged.

3

Rosslyn couldn't believe it. Her entire day consisted of bringing him coffee, getting him lunch, calling Laura and asking how she was doing. Did her uncle do anything for himself? She really shouldn't complain, because she was getting paid to do this. But call Aunt Laura? That was ridiculous.

There was a time difference Rosslyn had forgotten.

Aunt Laura said in a belittling tone, "You're from a small town. I don't expect you to understand how the rest of us live."

If she meant that as an insult, she missed the mark. Rosslyn was proud of where she came from and who she was. She didn't need some . . . rich bitch's approval. She spoke to Aunt Laura and Uncle Maxwell out of respect, not because they had earned it. *And definitely not because I'm afraid of you either.*

When Rosslyn was young that hadn't been the case. She remembered coming to the city with her parents, and Aunt Laura had been so mean. She had been upset they couldn't go to the restaurant she wanted because of how they were

28

dressed. Her father hadn't worn a suit jacket and tie, and her mother had been dressed equally casual. It was a family vacation and her parents were shown all the sites. Rosslyn might have only been seven at the time, but somehow her memories of that trip were as vivid as though it were yesterday.

I wish Mom was well enough to travel.

"Are you listening to me?" Laura snapped.

No. I wasn't. "I'm sorry Aunt Laura, I was multi-tasking."

"I asked if you knew what whore my husband took to the event last night."

Whore? It was evident last night that her uncle had a wondering eye, but could he actually be cheating? *Nothing would surprise me.* "Me."

"What did you say?" Laura asked.

"He took me." *I'm the whore.* She couldn't help but snicker, thinking of the look on her aunt's face.

"Wow, he really is losing his mind. You must have had a horrendous time."

"Actually, no. It was very enlightening." Hopefully that was vague enough.

"It seems he's getting desperate. I better get back to New York before he starts picking vagrants off the street. Besides, I'm growing tired of Paris."

Oh poor you. All you have to do is shop and eat all day. "I'm sure he'll be happy to have you home."

"Oh, my dear, you really are clueless. Tell him I'll be back in a few days."

"You don't want to tell him yourself?" *Talk like normal married people do?* She asked but already knew the answer. If there was love between them, she didn't see it. They were married in name only. *For richer or richer, for better, or the next best thing, till one of us croaks. Really romantic.*

29

Laura said, "I'll text him when I'm free." Then she ended the call.

Rosslyn was left missing her parents even more. They were supposed to be her family and she got nicer greetings from a perfect stranger. She grabbed her purse and cell phone and headed outside. It was her lunch break and even though her feet were killing her, she needed to put some distance between her and anything Grayson.

She remembered a place by Times Square that had the best cheesecake she'd ever eaten. That's exactly what she needed right now. That and to talk to her dad.

Rosslyn ordered, and called while waiting.

"Hello there, sweet pea. How are Uncle Max and Aunt Laura treating you?"

Probably the same as they always treated you. "Fine. I'm all settled in and started working already."

"Wow. That's my girl. You mother wants to know if you're eating well."

Rosslyn chuckled because the waitress just showed up with a piece of cheesecake that could feed six. "Having lunch now."

"I'm glad you're doing okay. I have to admit, I was worried about you going there all alone."

She understood why. Aunt Laura was right, Rosslyn was a small town girl, but what she failed to mention was how spirited small town girls were. Nothing kept them down for long.

"It's just a job like any other one, Dad."

"But you're working for Uncle Max."

"Actually he just tells me what to do and I do it."

"I didn't know you knew anything about contracts or construction."

She laughed. "Nope but I do about coffee and laundry.

He's starting me off slow. I'm sure before you know it, I'll be—"

"Bullshit. That's not what you're there for. You're capable of so much more. I'll call him and set him straight."

"Dad, please don't. I'm a grown woman and I know how to handle myself. Besides, I don't mind having an easy job. It pays the same without any stress."

"You always look on the bright side. Don't let them change you," he said firmly.

"Never, Dad. I'll always be your sweet pea. But I have to go or I won't have time to eat. I love you," she said, holding back her tears.

"I love you too."

She ended the call before she broke down. Rosslyn had wanted to ask how her mother was doing, but since her father didn't put her on the phone, it meant she was having a rough day. When you lived with someone long enough, you picked up on what was not said very easily. It was breaking her heart not to be home helping. Without her there, her father had to do it all on his own.

I'm sorry, Dad. I wish there was another way. Hopefully she could earn enough money in a few months to really make a difference.

"Miss, is everything okay?" the waitress asked.

Rosslyn wiped her tear-streaked face and nodded. "Thank you. Do you think I could get this to go?" She had lost her appetite.

"Of course." She took the cheesecake away and returned it in a takeout container.

She paid her bill and started toward the door, unfortunately someone was blocking her way intentionally. "If you don't mind, I'd like to pass."

"How is it I've never see you before and now I see you everywhere?"

It was a thought that crossed her mind as well. It made sense that she'd see him in a five-star restaurant, but this was a burger joint, one she could afford. What was he doing there? If he worked for Lawson Steel, maybe he lived on a budget as well, and the other guy he'd been with was his boss. She didn't have a detective's mind, which is probably why her uncle didn't give her a research job. But she had to know, so Rosslyn asked, "Should I be concerned that you're following me?" There was a small part of her that was serious. She was naïve to some of the things that took place in the city. She hoped to keep it that way too.

He laughed. "Stalking is not my thing."

It almost slipped past her lips. *What is?* That would open a longer conversation than she wanted to have with him. Yesterday she'd gotten out of there without Max knowing they spoke. But this was a popular place and anyone from Grayson Corp could be there. She didn't need someone ratting her out over something purely innocent.

If she was back home and a man as attractive as this guy wanted to chat up a storm with her, she'd have gotten all weak in the knees. Although he looked spectacular in a suit and tux, she couldn't help but wonder what he'd look like in a pair of jeans. She liked a guy who wasn't afraid to get his hands dirty with some hard physical work.

She was getting herself all steamed up thinking of him swinging an axe, chopping wood for the fireplace. *The only thing he probably lifts is weights at the gym.* "In that case, then you won't mind stepping out of my way," Rosslyn said.

He stepped aside slightly and said, "We didn't get a chance to introduce ourselves last night."

"And still no time today." It was a tight squeeze and she

turned her back to him as she brushed past him. Even through all those damn clothes, she could feel how fit he was. She didn't want to think about him at all, but evidently, he wasn't so easy to forget. *You're not only a distraction, but a risk I can't afford to take.* She wasn't here to date or anything else for that matter. Rosslyn needed to keep her mind where it belonged: keeping Uncle Max happy so she continued to get paid.

As she made her way through the busy street, she knew she better pick up the pace. If she rushed, she'd make it back to the office and never even have been missed. *Mostly because I'm not really needed.*

Rosslyn couldn't help but look over her shoulder. With how persistent he was, she wouldn't have been surprised to see him following her. She knew she should tell Max about this, but really, she didn't owe him anything. At least nothing she wasn't being paid for.

And that's what you get when you don't even want to admit to anyone that we're related.

Charles walked over to the table she had just left. He noticed the receipt out in the open. Everything in him said don't do it. But he wasn't out to snag her credit card number, just her name. There were other ways of obtaining the same information, but this was the easiest.

Picking up the paper he scanned it quickly. R. Clark. That wasn't much to go on and really, it was possible it wasn't even her card. If he wanted to know who she was, all he needed to do was backtrack people both he and Maxwell had spoken to last night. Surely one of those people would remember her name. *If Maxwell had the decency to introduce her.* He wasn't banking on that one.

Charles put the receipt back on the table and walked over to grab his takeout order. Once again that woman was distracting him from more important things. The only thing she offered was something he wasn't interested in. But somehow that didn't stop him from thinking about her.

For a woman in her position, he'd have thought she'd be more . . . free with her time to talk. He could've been a potential client. But she couldn't seem to get away from him fast enough. Charles didn't consider himself a stud, but women usually found him easy on the eyes. So what was her problem? Had Maxwell hired her to be exclusive?

With her stunning looks, that wouldn't surprise him one bit. And it also would explain her resistance to speak with him. *Don't want to rock the boat and lose your meal ticket.*

It was a shame, because if he'd met her elsewhere, Charles might have asked her out. There was no doubt he was attracted to her physically. A guy would have to be dead not to be. He didn't like snarky women, but she wasn't that either. She just seemed steadfast on what she wanted. He could respect that even if he didn't approve of her means for obtaining it.

But he wasn't done with her. Somehow that woman connected to Maxwell and might be another piece in the puzzle to help take him down. Not that he wanted to know what their pillow talk was, but Maxwell was one who liked to brag, especially to a smoking hot woman like that. Maxwell probably never gave her credit for anything more than her looks. Charles already could tell there was a lot more to her than that. Too bad she was wasting it.

As they handed him his bag, Charles laughed to himself. *Seems we both felt like cheesecake for lunch.* He didn't want to know what else they had in common. The more he knew about her, the more he'd feel guilty using her.

Heading back to the office, he pulled out his cell phone and called Gareth.

"Two days in a row? This isn't like you, Charles. Maxwell getting under your skin that much?" Gareth asked upon answering.

"I need information on a name."

Gareth's tone changed. "You've come to the right person. What's the name?"

"R. Clark."

There was silence on the line. Then he heard Gareth huff. "Please tell me you have more than that."

"I thought you said you were efficient."

"And I thought you wanted my help," Gareth snarled.

He didn't want to open up a line of questions, but there was no way around it. "Do you remember the woman from The Choice?"

"You mean the waitress who came on to me?"

"No."

"The redhead who handed me her number when we were leaving?" Gareth tried again.

"The blonde."

Gareth laughed. "You know I'm not into blondes. Well, I still date them, but they're not my favorite. I prefer—"

"Gareth, I'm not asking you to rate the woman, just get me information on her." Charles was losing his patience again. This was becoming a habit that he didn't like. Gathering himself, he said in a more controlled tone, "She was sitting with Maxwell. I want to know everything you can find on her."

"What does that have to do with what you're working on? I thought you wanted to ruin his company, not steal his mistress."

Gareth's sense of humor was really getting on Charles's

nerves, more now for some odd reason. Growling out, Charles said, "I don't care who she is Gareth, I only want to know what she knows. Either you can get me information or not."

"I think you're wasting your time if you think Maxwell would divulge any information to a call girl. Granted, he's done some stupid shit, but why would he tell her anything?"

Because a man could get lost in those blue eyes of hers. "I'm not saying he did, but I think it's worth exploring."

"You don't want me to ask her?" Gareth asked.

"No. Just get me her contact information. I'll do the rest."

Gareth laughed. "You do know I'm much better with the ladies than you are."

"And I know you'll forget what I'm looking for too." Gareth definitely liked brunettes, but Charles knew when it came to the opposite sex, Gareth easily could be pulled off task.

"You say that now. We'll see what happens."

"What the hell does that mean?" Charles snapped.

"I saw the way you looked at her. Wasn't even sure you had noticed Maxwell sitting there."

"Don't go there. I miss nothing when it comes to Maxwell." *I'm not going to be blindsided like our father was.* It had almost cost him everything. Could they have survived without Lawson Steel? Yes. But this had been a family run business since the early 1800s. You don't let go of something like that without a fight. And Maxwell was going to get one.

"I'll have it to you by the end of the day," Gareth said and ended the call.

Charles had no idea how Gareth pulled this stuff off, but Gareth hadn't let him down yet. Whether or not he obtained everything legally was another story. But Gareth had friends in high places. People who would have access to things the average person didn't. And as far as Charles was concerned, the less he knew, the better.

As soon as he walked into his office he saw Dylan behind his desk, occupying his chair. "What the hell do you think you're doing?" *Try it out, but this office is not yours.*

"We need to talk," Dylan said.

"Get out of my chair and let's talk." Charles put the lunch on the desk and walked around till Dylan vacated his seat. He didn't think Dylan would go looking in his drawers. There were things in there he wasn't ready to share yet. First of all, the contract his father made him sign. If any of them knew of its existence, they would start to question everything he asked of them. Their father meant well, but it could cause a wedge between them all that even time wouldn't heal. Once the trust was gone, it was gone for good.

Dylan got up and took the seat across from Charles. "I heard you hired all the interns. Wasn't that supposed to be something we *all* decided on? Unless I'm missing something, you might be the CEO, but the rest of us are partners in this company."

This had nothing to do with the interns. Dylan was still pissed off about the contract being denied. "You might want to go knock on Seth's door then, because he did the research and hiring of this group of individuals."

Dylan leaned back in his seat and said, "Is it just me you don't trust to make decisions then? From what I can see, Seth has free rein to do what he wants, and Gareth, well, who the hell knows what he does."

"Probably the same thing as Jordan and Ethan, their jobs. Why don't you just tell me what you really came here to discuss?"

"I talked to Dad last night."

Charles didn't see that one coming. Dad was the last

person any of them went to. Usually because it came with a long-winded explanation of how they needed to figure it out themselves. Even as grown-ass adults, the response hadn't changed any. Maybe it was because of what he'd been through, but as far as guidance, they were left on their own.

"And now you're in *my* office."

"He said you have a lot going on. Makes me think there is something you haven't told us. Want to come clean now or explain yourself when I find out on my own?"

Dylan was no fool. Charles probably could hide things from the others easier. If he hadn't needed Gareth's help, he wouldn't know anything either. But Dylan wasn't going to let this drop.

"You know how I feel about Maxwell Grayson," Charles said.

Nodding, Dylan said, "It'd be hard to miss. You loathe the guy. What I don't get is why. Every company has competition. Hell, it's healthy. Keeps a person driving hard."

"That is does. But there are things you don't know about our competitor."

Dylan said, "I'm well aware of his reputation."

"Most people are. But there are things you're not aware of. Do you have to be anywhere because this might take a while?"

He cocked a brow, pulled out his cell phone, and sent a text. "Not anymore."

Charles spent the next few hours not just going through what Maxwell had pulled with their father, but all the other unethical shit he'd gotten away with over the years. Alone it didn't look like much, but when compiled together, Maxwell was just a well-dressed, rich thug.

He could tell by Dylan's expression that he was angry. "Now you understand why I've been so . . . evasive lately."

"I do. What I don't understand is why Dad never told any of us?"

It always seemed that Charles was the favorite. The truth was, he was just the oldest. Their father entrusted him with things he didn't ask for or want, but it just naturally came that way.

"Guess when you're dragged around to meetings all the time when you're a kid, you hear things others don't. Consider yourself lucky."

"Why? If I'd have known, I'd have done something about it long before now."

"Exactly," Charles replied. "He would've expected it. Hell, he might still. But we are older, wiser and . . . six. Fucking with us would be stupid." *And deadly.* Charles never would allow anything to happen to his family.

Dylan said, "Let me guess, you don't want the others to know."

"When the time is right, we'll tell them. Right now, it's about making sure no stone is left unturned." Charles was leaving nothing to chance. Maxwell had gotten away with shit for far too long. This time he was going to find himself cornered and the gig would be up.

Maxwell, you're going to regret ever fucking with a Lawson. Charles just wished his father had handled it long ago. But at least, hopefully soon, it would be over.

4

Rosslyn thought after a few days on the job, she'd be given more responsibility. That wasn't the case at all. She was tempted to talk to her uncle about it, let him know she wasn't an idiot and really was capable of following directions. She was sure in his mind that would mean making the coffee and not just taking it to him.

At least Aunt Laura was supposed to come into the office shortly. Their phone conversation hadn't gone very well, but maybe things would be different in person.

Liz, her uncle's secretary, came over and asked, "Do you want to have lunch today?"

Was she hearing things? Someone was actually talking directly to her without wanting something? With a great big smile she replied, "I'd love to. Where do you want to go?"

"Anywhere not in the building," Liz said. Rosslyn cocked a brow. In a softer voice Liz added, "Trust me, you don't want to be anywhere close when she gets here."

"Who?"

"Mrs. Grayson." Liz shook her head. "I've been here for

ten years, and it is the same thing every time. It wouldn't surprise me if they kill each other someday."

Rosslyn's eyes widened. "That bad?" She couldn't believe they'd act in such a manner, especially at his business.

"It's getting worse, not better. I don't want to be a witness to anything said or done."

It was evident things weren't good between the two. Softly Rosslyn asked, "Then why do they stay together?"

Liz snickered. "Money. It always comes down to money."

Not for everyone. "That's . . . very sad."

"I hear the Grayson family was all the same. At least he is the end of the line."

In name, yes. But she was a Grayson by blood. The Graysons no one ever spoke about, obviously. Even Liz, someone who worked closely with Uncle Max, didn't know of their existence. She wasn't sure if that should please her or not. The only thing Rosslyn was sure of was being a Clark seemed beneficial. Maybe not financially, but at least in things that mattered like charity, kindness and . . . *true love*.

It was important at times like this. With her mother's health slipping, it took a man who truly loved his wife to stand by her. Parkinson's had been something she didn't know anything about. But once her mother had been diagnosed with it, she read every article and so-called medical breakthrough to be found. Unfortunately, everything treated the symptoms, but nothing was a cure.

She didn't want to discuss Max with Liz or anyone else. She was afraid her opinion of him wasn't any better. Rosslyn also knew where she didn't want to go. Anyplace where *he* could be. Of course, that wasn't easy for her to guess. "I'm not from around here. Where could we go that many people don't know about?"

Liz laughed. "I know all the best hiding places. How do you think I've been able to survive this place for so long?"

Rosslyn was surprised how freely she was speaking negatively about her boss. Though Rosslyn wasn't a fan of Max either, she wouldn't partake in boss bashing. It wasn't her style.

Liz reached into the bottom drawer of her desk and said, "I just heard she entered the building. This is our chance to make a run for it before it's too late."

Rosslyn was feeling guilty, as though she should be there to greet her aunt. "I need to make a stop in the ladies' room. How about I meet you in the lobby in ten minutes?"

"Make it on the corner across from the coffee shop and you have a deal. The longer I'm in this building, the more likely I'll be trapped." Liz scurried down the hall and didn't even take the elevator.

Really? She couldn't believe Liz was taking the stairs to avoid Laura. Rosslyn tried to prepare herself for whatever her aunt had to say. She held her breath as the elevator doors opened. Laura strutted down the hallway in her direction. She could already see her aunt's expression and she wasn't happy.

"You must be the little tart of the month."

Rosslyn cleared her throat and said, "No, I'm . . . the new personal assistant." She couldn't believe her aunt didn't recognize her. Each Christmas her parents had sent them a card with a family photo. She may look a bit different but not that much. Besides, they had spoken on the phone two days ago. Could she really be that daft? *No. She just doesn't care about anyone but herself.*

"I don't want to know what you assist him with."

Rosslyn shivered at the thought. *I should've listened to Liz and gotten the hell out of here.* "I was about to go to lunch, unless there is something you need first."

"The only thing I need is to see my husband and give him a piece of my mind."

Laura stormed into Max's office and slammed the door behind her. Sure enough, the sparks starting flying between them with shouts echoing down the hall. Rosslyn went to her desk, grabbed her purse, and rushed to the elevator before she heard too much. It was worse for her than for Liz. This wasn't just her boss and his wife arguing, this was her dysfunctional family.

When she made it outside and caught up with Liz, she saw her talking to a man. Liz was laughing and flirting up a storm. Rosslyn didn't want to interrupt but didn't want to blow Liz off either. So she walked up and before she could say a word Liz said, "Oh, I thought you changed your mind. Would you mind if Sam came with us?"

She wasn't looking forward to lunch with Liz anymore, never mind adding another person. Right now all she wanted was to go someplace where she didn't need to think about Grayson Corp. "I was just about to ask if I could take a rain check."

Liz didn't seem upset in the least. "Definitely. Maybe tomorrow." Then she watched Liz link arms with Sam as they disappeared into the crowd.

Rosslyn had no idea where to go, but she knew it wasn't going to be back to Grayson Corp. The closest place was the coffee shop across the street. It wasn't what she was in the mood for, but it was quick and within her budget.

Stepping off the curb, a car horn blew, scaring her half to death. She was in the right. The walk signal was on and she was in the crosswalk. Rosslyn had no idea what overcame her, but she slapped the hood of the car and said sharply, "Watch where you're going."

Even though he had been in the wrong, it still was a ballsy

thing to do. It didn't take long for her to realize just how foolish her action had been. The man got out of his car and approached her, swearing and waving a fist in the air. Her heart raced. How she wished she had ruby slippers to click together and wake up back home. But nothing was going to get her out of this situation.

She couldn't believe people were still walking across the street as though nothing was happening. If the man had hit her, knocked her out, would they just step over her body? Rosslyn wasn't sure, but she needed to do something, and apologizing sounded like a good place to start.

Raising her hands she said, "Sir, I'm sorry. I didn't mean to . . . touch your car. I was caught off guard and . . . I'm—"

"Take another step toward her, and the only ride you're getting is in an ambulance. Got it?"

Even though she didn't know his name, she knew that voice. But Rosslyn wasn't about to take her eyes off the man who had been approaching her. His focus was no longer on her but on the man behind her. At first it looked like he was going to challenge that threat, but something made him change his mind.

She heard him swearing under his breath as he walked back to his car and got inside. Rosslyn stepped back onto the sidewalk and finally turned around. "Thank you, but I was handling it myself."

"If what you mean by handling it is about to get knocked on your ass, then yeah, you were doing fine."

That's not exactly the way she saw it, but then again, she wasn't sure either. Rosslyn had been scared more than she wanted to admit. But having him come to her rescue kind of threw her as well. In such a big city, why did they keep bumping into each other?

"I guess I'm still getting used to how things are done here."

"Have lunch with me and I'll give you a few pointers to keep you safe."

She debated accepting or not. Rosslyn wanted to talk to him. It was ridiculous because they really didn't know each other. Yet in the few days she's been here, she'd spoken more to him than anyone she knew. Maybe if they had lunch, he wouldn't be a stranger anymore. Max had said she shouldn't speak to him, but it was possible he was only referring to that one night, not forever. Besides, Max had no right controlling who she spoke to. He didn't own her. As long as she didn't talk about Max or Grayson Corp, she didn't see any harm in having lunch with him.

"I don't even know your name."

"Charles. And you are?"

"I'm Rosslyn." This was better. At least she wasn't going off with a complete stranger. Just one who seemed to appear everywhere she was. "Okay," she said.

"Okay?" He actually looked surprised. *Not as much as I am I bet.* She really couldn't believe she was going to do this. Then he repeated with a smile, "Okay."

"Do you want to go across the street to the café?"

Charles shook his head. "I know this place that has the best cheesecake."

"I do too. We bumped into each other there two days ago." Not that she could forget any time they crossed paths.

"That place is good, but this one is amazing. It's a bit of a ways. Are you in a rush to get back to work?" Charles asked.

Normally she'd say yes, but Liz was correct. What was an extra half hour? "I have until two."

"Perfect." Charles waved for a taxi and one pulled right to the curb.

How was that? She sometimes stood hailing a taxi and thought she must be invisible. Then again standing next to him . . .

While they drove, Charles actually held up his end and gave her a lecture about the do's and dont's in the city. Most of it was common sense.

"I really don't know what came over me. I'm not that type of person. Usually everything rolls off my shoulders and I let it go. But there was a look in his eyes, like he wasn't even sorry that he almost hit me. And I . . . lost my temper."

"That's you losing your temper?"

She knew it didn't seem like much, but for her, it was. Rosslyn didn't go around slapping hoods of vehicles and yelling. "Guess I'm more of a quiet person."

Charles laughed. "It's good to let it out every once in a while. Just next time don't take on a car. They usually win."

"I was more worried about the man. He really was upset." Rosslyn shivered with the thought of what could've happened if Charles hadn't backed the guy down. "I'm not sure I thanked you."

"If I hadn't stepped in, I'm sure someone else would've."

She wasn't so sure, but she hoped he was right. "Well there won't be a next time. I'll never be so reckless again."

The taxi came to a halt and Charles said, "They also have the best pasta here too."

She hadn't been paying attention to where they had gone, but obviously they weren't in the city any longer. "Is this a diner?"

"It is."

"How on earth did you ever find this place?" Rosslyn asked.

"A college buddy of mine. His parents own it. Heck, his parents are the cooks. Everything is homemade."

As soon as they entered, a short well-rounded older woman called out. "Charlie. I was wondering when you'd be back." Then she peered around him and gave Rosslyn the once over. With a bright smile she asked, "Ah. Who is this lovely creature?"

Rosslyn felt as though she was walking into someone's home instead of a restaurant. *Now this I like.* "Hi. I'm Rosslyn Clark."

"Well Rosslyn, any friend of Charlie's is a friend of ours. Come. Sit. I'll get you some lasagna and garlic bread."

She didn't wait for them to respond before heading into the back. Charles asked, "How about the table in the corner?"

Rosslyn looked over. "It says reserved."

"That's because it's held for family and friends."

She noticed it was the best table in the place, secluded yet you could see everything. As they waited she said, "Guess you're not getting your cheesecake today."

"Oh yes we are. But you have to eat first. Mama's rules. No dessert before lunch."

Rosslyn giggled. "I'm sure she would make an exception for *Charlie.*"

He cocked a brow. "You're not going to start calling me that too, are you?"

"I don't know. I kind of like it. Not so stuffy. Charles is a serious name but Charlie . . . well he likes to have fun."

Charles laughed. "Stuffy? Well I guess that does describe me."

"Charlie, you are not stuffy. Sometimes a bit too serious, but not stuffy," Mama said as she brought them their food. "Now how about a glass of wine?"

"Not for me. Maybe water with lemon?" Rosslyn said.

Mama shook her head. "Now who is stuffy?"

Rosslyn smiled. "Wine would be wonderful, thank you."

"Mama, not so much food. We are trying to save room for your famous cheesecake," Charles said.

Mama looked at Rosslyn and said, "She is all skin and bone. You need to feed her more. Then you have dessert."

Mama left them again at the table. "She means it too."

Rosslyn said, "That I'm too skinny?"

"No. That we're not getting dessert unless we finish our lunch. She's tough."

She picked up her fork and said, "Then I guess we better start because this portion is huge."

"You got lucky, this is small. You should see what I get when I come alone. She must think I never eat."

"I'd burst if I had to eat more than this."

"But one bite and you won't be able to stop. Trust me, they are the best."

Funny, trusting him seemed to be something she was doing. He really didn't seem like a bad guy. She wondered why Uncle Max wanted her to stay away from him. *Maybe because he's nice and Uncle Max doesn't like nice people.* That very well could be the reason. There was another option. One she didn't want to think about. *Assholes can pick out other assholes in a crowd.*

She really hoped Charles wasn't like Uncle Max. Rosslyn really could use a friend in New York City. Could that be Charles? Probably not. He didn't seem like a friends-only type. Then again, was there anything wrong with wanting something more? As long as they were both in agreement, and neither set any expectations, what was wrong with having a bit of . . . fun.

Rosslyn snickered to herself. *Cause you're not the casual anything type Rosslyn. You're the all or nothing type.* She knew she couldn't date someone like Charles, but Charlie on the other hand, he had potential.

"You seem to be enjoying your food."

She looked up from her plate. "Sorry, I was just thinking of something."

"I figured because her lasagna never made me laugh before. Care to share the joke?"

She felt her cheeks warm. "Not today."

Charles grinned. "I like that."

"That I won't share it?"

He shook his head. "Not today makes me hope that we will do this again sometime. How about Friday night?"

Charles was asking her out. A planned date. What if he wanted to take her to one of those fancy places like The Choice? She didn't have a huge wardrobe to pick from. And she really wouldn't enjoy herself either. But she did want to see him. "If it's here again, I'm in."

That eliminated the need to shop for something new. Something she couldn't afford. Any money spent out of her pocket was less going home to her parents.

"It's a date. But I suggest you not eat anything that day. Friday nights she goes all out."

Rosslyn smiled. "Then I'll be sure to wear stretchable clothing too."

"And comfortable shoes. If it's nice, we can take a walk around the neighborhood. They always have some music playing somewhere. No official bands, just . . . well, you'll see."

She really was looking forward to it. Rosslyn was missing the comforts of home, and Charles somehow was giving them to her. "Sounds nice. I'm really not into all the hustle and bustle of the city."

"Where are you from?"

"Alexandria Bay."

"I've heard of it. Never been, but I hear it's beautiful."

"It is. I love being near the water. My father owns a small marina repair shop. He can fix just about any engine there is." At least he had until her mother became too sick to be alone. Rosslyn was staying home and helping out all she could. And they had a certified nursing assistant come in a few times a week as well. But her mother couldn't be left alone anymore. Her dementia, yet just another horrible side of the Parkinson's, had gotten worse. For some unknown reason, she became angry when Rosslyn tried to help her. It broke Rosslyn's heart, but it was best for her parents that she not be there as often as she had been. So all that was left for Rosslyn to do to help was make enough money so her father could afford to stay home and care for her mother.

"And here you are, out chasing your dreams in the city," Charles said.

She shook her head. "No. But it pays the bills. Guess that's why we all are here, right?"

Before he could answer, Mama had returned. "Looks like you both enjoyed your lunch. Should I bring over coffee and dessert now?"

Rosslyn didn't have any room, not even for dessert. "Nothing for me. I couldn't eat another bite."

Mama put her hands on her hips and shook her head. "You don't know what you're missing."

Charles said, "Actually Mama, we need to get back to work. Do you think you could package up two to go?"

She seemed happy to do that, but said, "Charlie, I keep telling you that you need to have fun. Let someone else do the work. Take a vacation. Take your young lady with you."

"Mama, you know it's not that simple. And I don't see your son Sal slowing down either."

Mama huffed and started muttering things in Italian. "Salvatore is just like you. How am I ever going to have a grandson to rock if all he does is work?" She threw her hands up in the air and walked away muttering all over again.

Charles turned back to Rosslyn and said, "Good, now she'll be calling and nagging him instead of me."

Rosslyn's eyes widened. "That's horrible. You just threw your friend under the bus."

"Sal's done it to me more times than I can count."

"Oh, Charlie. I guess you're really not that stuffy after all," she teased.

"Keep it up and I'll show you just how wild I can be," Charles warned.

Oh I bet you can get wilder than I can imagine. Once again, her mind went where it shouldn't. She had no intentions of having sex with this man, but those dark eyes of his and his sexy husky voice were teasing. That tall muscular physique didn't hurt either. Why was it that what you know you shouldn't do, was always the most tempting? *And doing Charles would definitely be a sweet escape from my reality.*

But she couldn't afford to drift too far into the wonderful world of fantasy. It would only add a complication she couldn't allow right now. But a date here and there, what harm could come of that?

Teasing she said, "I'm not worried. I'm sure Mama will keep you in check."

Charles let out a soft growl. "Unfortunately, that's true."

Gareth had provided Charles with some information, but Rosslyn was forthcoming with much of it herself. But if Gareth hadn't told him she actually worked for Maxwell, he never would've been lingering around that area. Normally he stayed as far away from the Grayson Corp building as he could. Even at the event on Sunday, they didn't speak. Maxwell was no fool, he knew Charles despised him. Hopefully that was all he knew.

What Charles didn't understand was what the hell possessed him to take Rosslyn to Mama's. The sole purpose of being that close was to see what she knew. Learning she was Maxwell's personal assistant was like hitting the jackpot. If anyone knew stuff, she would. But why would someone who appeared to be so damn nice work for such an asshole? Someone like Maxwell probably hired her thinking he could get a little extra something on the side. After spending a little time with her, Charles didn't think that was the case. And Mama was a good judge of character too. If Mama thought for a second Rosslyn was some little tart, as she called them, she never would've been so warm and friendly.

But just because Rosslyn wasn't Maxwell's lover, didn't mean her loyalty didn't lie with that guy. He signed her paychecks after all. Rosslyn spoke about a lot of things on their drive back into the city. Not once did she mention work or Maxwell. Heck, she even had the taxi driver let her off down the street from Grayson Corp. Did she not want him to know where she worked? Because if so, it was too late.

At least he didn't need to work on accidently bumping into her again. She gave him her cell phone number, which would save a hell of a lot of time. And since they were going out Friday, it gave Charles some time to think of something other than her.

Like that was really going to happen. That was two days away and the scent of her perfume lingering in the taxi was still driving him crazy. He found her . . . intoxicating. It was very difficult not to ask her why she worked there and, hell, even offer her a job at Lawson Steel. Until he knew exactly what was going on, he'd only allow himself to get so close. For all he knew, she was the enemy.

"So you're really taking her out?" Gareth asked. "Like on a date?"

"Not a date. This is business. You know that."

Gareth laughed. "Those are the famous last words of every man before he falls. You might be able to fool the others, but I know you, Charles. Business doesn't involved wining and dining someone. Besides, you already have what you want. You know she works for him."

Don't remind me. Charles didn't care who worked for Maxwell. So why did it bother him that Rosslyn did? Probably the same reason it went up his ass that they had lunch together or were at the event together. Charles was attracted to her. But that wouldn't, or at least shouldn't, cloud his judgment.

Gareth was starting to piss him off. "Don't you have something better to do?"

"Most definitely, but nothing half as fun as giving you shit," Gareth said. "Besides, what good is it to confide in me if you don't want my help to keep you on track?"

"Is this what you call help? Because right now all I hear is you flapping your lips with nothing useful coming out." Charles knew he could trust Gareth, as he could all his brothers. But Gareth was usually easier to talk to. Today, that wasn't the case. He almost wished it was Dylan he'd called. Which reminded him. "Have you spoken to Dylan lately?"

"How do you define lately?"

"Since Monday."

"No. I spoke to Dad and he said Dylan was upset. I figured the two of you were going at it again, and I wanted to stay out of it. Let me guess, you told him no and he's not taking that lying down."

"That pretty much sums it up. But there is more. He knows what I'm doing."

"You mean regarding Maxwell?" Gareth asked.

"Yes."

"Fuck. After lecturing me not to say one fucking word, you do."

He couldn't argue with Gareth there. "Dylan didn't leave me much choice. He swore not to say a word to the others. But once we are ready to make our move, we will have to clue them all in."

"No shit. Because when Maxwell goes batshit crazy on revenge, each of us will have a target on our back. That's why I want you to have all the facts before you act. If not, we're all fucked."

Charles knew that. Maxwell would go after Lawson Steel full force. Would he do more than just go after the company? That was something none of them knew. The last pieces of the puzzle were knowing how dirty his hands were and how wide his reach. "Don't worry, when I go to the feds, he won't be able to back pedal or buy his way out of it."

"I sure as hell hope not. Otherwise, it's going to make what happened to Dad look like a beach party."

Only Charles knew how deeply that had affected their father. The money was only one piece. He had lost his fight. When Charles asked him what was wrong, his father wouldn't answer. His reputation being questioned had crushed his father. And Charles was damn sure his grandfather had some choice words about it as well. If anything, his grandfather probably made his father feel as though he was getting what he deserved. No one deserved to be treated like that. Well, maybe Maxwell. *And maybe my grandfather too.*

For now he listened, learned, and waited. The time was approaching, but it couldn't be rushed. He hadn't thought too much about the people working for Maxwell, but now he needed to. Charles didn't want one innocent person getting caught in the crossfire. Especially if that person was Rosslyn.

5

"Are you sure you don't want to go out for dinner?" Liz asked.

"Yes, really. I've got plans."

"You're not just saying that because I ditched you for Sam on Wednesday are you?"

Rosslyn shook her head. "I enjoyed my lunch just fine. Maybe not as much as you did. I can't believe you were gone so long."

Liz blushed. "We used to date and broke up a few months back. It was over something so stupid."

It was none of her business, but for some strange reason, Liz seemed to want to talk to her about it.

"Sam hates me working for Grayson Corp. See, he is on the construction side of things. And he and his brother used to work for the company. But Sam is the type that questions everything. Guess he asked the wrong question and the next thing he knew, he was fired. So was his brother."

"I can understand how that would put a strain on a relationship."

"It wouldn't have been so bad, except for how closely I

work with Mr. Grayson. But now he sees that I'm just doing my job. And quitting because of what happened to him wouldn't make anything better. If anything, it'd drive us further apart."

"Why don't you give him a call? Maybe you guys should go out tonight," Rosslyn suggested.

"I don't want him to think I'm pushing him to get back together."

"Is that what you want?" she asked.

Liz nodded. "He's all I've been able to think about."

"I've always found it's better to be up front and honest about your feelings. The fear of what could happen usually is unwarranted. I'm sure Sam had his own set of concerns too."

"You're right. He said that after breaking it off, he thought I hated him and moved on. God, he was so wrong. I cried for weeks, not just days. And the only date I went on was with someone down in accounting and that wasn't really a date. We went to a company party together."

"Then it sounds like you and Sam need time together to work things out. And more time than you can get on your lunch break." Which had gone over by a lot. Thankfully Max and Laura were still too busy fighting to have noticed. Things seemed to have quieted down a bit, but not much. Each time Laura came around, everyone was on edge and ran for the hills.

"I guess I'll see you on Monday," Liz said as she headed toward the bus stop.

Good luck. She really liked Liz and now understood why she wasn't fond of her dear ol' uncle. Liz was doing what she had to in order to pay her bills, no different that Rosslyn.

She made a mental note to get to know Liz better. It sucked that Liz was opening up to her in a way she never would if she had a clue Rosslyn was related to Max. *Heck, no one would like me.*

Rosslyn wondered if Charles would feel the same way. She hadn't told Charles she worked for Grayson Corp. What if his boss didn't want him talking with the competition either? She had a feeling Charles did what he wanted to, but she didn't want to get him in trouble. After hearing what happened to Sam, Rosslyn realized it didn't take much around here to be fired.

She didn't believe her uncle would do that to her, but then again, what would stop him? He didn't care enough about his own sister to ask how she was. *I don't think you know how sick she is.*

Rosslyn looked at her watch and knew her father would be cooking dinner right now. She tried not to call him unless she had to. That last thing he needed was to worry about her. And if her mother was having a rough day, her father needed all his mental and physical strength to get through it as well.

So she opted to head home and change. Rosslyn had been lucky to find a cheap room for rent. The couple was traveling and needed someone to stay and watch their cat and apartment for a month. The timing was perfect, but one week had already passed. She needed to come up with a long-term plan for housing. Nothing in the city was going to be affordable. She couldn't talk to Charles about it because that would sound like she was asking him to move in. That definitely wasn't the case. So she made a list of topics to avoid tonight.

1. Work.
2. Housing
3. Family

That left hobbies, music, and food. That was plenty for

one date and probably more than they would have time for. It was dinner. She'd probably be home before dark. As Charles had suggested, she wore a pair of sneakers so if they did go for a walk, her feet wouldn't feel like they were on fire. Besides, she wasn't out to impress him. He'd already seen her at her best at the event. He might as well see her as she liked to be, in a pair of jeans with a casual top. Normally she'd have pulled her hair into a ponytail, but it wasn't long enough anymore.

Rosslyn's mother used to love her long hair. She wondered if she would notice she'd gotten it cut. The night before Rosslyn left to meet up with Uncle Max, her mother was so confused, Rosslyn wasn't even sure if she knew who she was. It was hard being away from her, but it was a blessing that her mother hardly knew she was gone.

She didn't want to stay away too long for fear her mother would forget her completely. Traveling back and forth wasn't cost effective, but she'd promised her father she would be home every other weekend. So having a date with Charles tonight would at least help ease the ache within her.

Rosslyn felt guilty for looking forward to him picking her up. Why should she be happy even for a minute? She tried fighting it, but she couldn't. She'd had a nice time with him a couple of days ago and wanted to feel that feeling again. *Alive.* Like the old Rosslyn before her mother had become ill. Playful, carefree, but most of all, happy.

Her phone rang and she answered, "Hello, is this Charlie?"

"Very funny. I'm going to be there in five minutes. Do you want me to come up or do you want to meet me in front of the building?"

Parking was not easy and she'd never ask him to come up. Not only because he'd probably get a ticket, but this wasn't her apartment. It was part of the agreement that no guests were allowed. Since she hadn't known anyone at that time, it'd never crossed her mind that it might become an issue.

"I'll be right down." She ended the call, found Snuggles, and gave her a couple of scratches behind the ears. "I promise, tonight you'll get a lot more." A few meows and Miss Snuggles curled back up as though she understood.

Rosslyn never had a pet before but in this short time she'd grown fond of having the cat around. It was companionship even if not human. And somehow the cat seemed to pick up on her emotions too. The first night Rosslyn had cried herself to sleep and the cat had stayed right by her side. *You probably are missing your family as much as I am mine.*

She needed to get out of there before she started feeling down again and decided to back out. Grabbing her purse, she headed down to meet Charles. He pulled up in a black sporty car that looked quite expensive. Once she got inside and felt the leather seats, she knew she was right. Not only did it look like luxury, it felt like it too.

As she looked over at him, concerned that she may have underdressed, she was pleased to find him dressed casually too. "Are we really going back to the same place tonight?"

He nodded. "Unless there is someplace else you'd prefer."

"No. That place is more my style. Makes me think of home."

"That's why I go there as well," Charles replied.

"You mean you're from a small town too?" Rosslyn hoped she could get him talking a bit more about himself this time.

"No. I'm actually from here."

"The city? Really?" He nodded. "Wow. I can't imagine

living here my whole life. I need trees and lakes and swimming holes."

"I can't give you all that tonight, but there is a park not far from the diner. They have a swing and maybe a slide."

Rosslyn laughed. "In a pinch, that'll do."

"And after eating tonight, we're going to need to do something physical."

A couple of things crossed her mind, but quickly she pushed them aside. *It's not going to happen. It can't happen.* "Maybe we should skip dessert then." He shot her a look of surprise. "Don't worry. I was only joking. That cheesecake was amazing." And probably enough calories to last her a week.

"You had me scared there for a minute."

"Afraid of Mama?"

"You better believe it. And if you were smart, you'd be too."

Rosslyn had a feeling Mama was all bark and no bite. Of course she wasn't about to put that theory to test. "Maybe she'd let us share one."

Once she said it she realized how intimate it sounded. But Charles's response didn't say he'd picked up on it. "I like a woman who knows how to negotiate a good deal."

"Don't be too impressed. I was only thinking about my wardrobe and how I can't afford to replace it all if it doesn't fit." Unfortunately that was truer than she'd like to admit. And being in his fancy car only reminded her of how he wouldn't understand that problem.

But it doesn't matter. This is just a distraction, nothing more.

Dinner at Mama's was excellent as always. But the usual

reserved table had been prepared differently than before. Mama had set a new linen tablecloth with a vase of fresh cut flowers. It was a good thing they actually showed up or he might be in the doghouse with Mama. She might not be family, but she accepted him as such. Because of that, Charles never would intentionally disappoint her.

There was another woman he also didn't want to disappoint. Rosslyn seemed very vulnerable for some reason. There were times, even though they were enjoying themselves, she seemed a million miles away. He saw it in her eyes. Something was troubling her, and it was driving him crazy. Asking her might ruin the part she was enjoying.

But Charles never got the chance to ask. Mama walked over to say goodnight to them and beat him to the punch. "My dear, you look sad. I hope this big goon has not said or done something to upset you."

Rosslyn shook her head. "No. He's a perfect gentleman."

That probably was the first time anyone had ever called him either of those. If he hadn't been concerned about Rosslyn, he'd have corrected her assessment of him.

Mama gave her a sympathetic look then turned her attention to him. "Charlie, you better treat her right. You don't find ladies like this anymore. If only my Salvatore could find one like her."

Rosslyn smiled and said, "I'm sure one day he'll show up with the right one."

Mama huffed. "He's never brought a girl here. And you're the first one our Charlie has brought here. Oh the joy that brings me." She leaned over and hugged Rosslyn then did the same to him. "Now go before I don't let you go."

Charles knew she meant it. There was no stopping her once she got started. And it always had to start at the beginning, when she first came to this country when she was four.

They would be there all night. Rosslyn might enjoy hearing them, but he probably could repeat the stories word for word.

"Tell Sal I said hi." Charles knew she'd be calling him once they left. And he also knew Sal would be calling him to curse him out shortly after. Charles hadn't meant to put the pressure on his friend, but it was on now.

Unfortunately, it wasn't real. This might be a date, but not with the hope that it would actually go anywhere. Once he dropped the dime on Grayson to the feds, Rosslyn, as well as most of the employees there, were going to hate him. Their livelihood was going to be affected. Charles wished there was something he could do to avoid that, but some things were out of his control.

Maxwell didn't give a shit about all the people who lost their jobs when he fucking lied about my father. That was the major difference. He wasn't Maxwell. And ne never wanted to be compared to him either. Would Rosslyn see the difference? Maybe not. But he was going to do everything he could not to hurt her in the process. *I don't want any collateral damage, especially not for her.*

As they left the restaurant, music was playing in the distance. The night was warm, not a cloud in the sky, and Rosslyn needed some distraction. So did he. It'd been a long time since he sat in the park and listened to the old-timers play. Actually so long that he wasn't sure if those guys were the same ones. There was only one way to find out.

"What do you say? Want to kick off our shoes and lie in the grass for a while?"

Rosslyn shot him a funny look. "Are you serious?"

"I am."

The joy in her eyes said it was exactly what she needed. "I'd love that."

Charles reached out and took her hand in his. As they

walked toward the commons, he said, "It's nice to see you smiling again."

"I've been smiling all night," Rosslyn stated.

"I mean really smiling."

"And you know the difference?" Rosslyn challenged.

I do with you. "You smile with your eyes."

She shook her head. "We've only met a couple of times and you can read my emotions in my eyes?" He nodded. She stopped and said, "Then tell me what I'm thinking right now."

Charles did as she said and looked into the most beautiful blue eyes he'd ever seen. They seemed to darken the longer he stared. Then he let her hand go, slipped his around her waist, and pulled her close. "They say you want me to kiss you until we don't know our names. But this will need to suffice." Before she could protest, he leaned over and kissed her.

Damn her lips were soft and tasty. He wanted more, so much more, but thankfully they were on the sidewalk and people were already beginning to talk. It was the old neighborhood after all. And it wouldn't take long before this little kiss made it back to Mama. Of course, by then they would tell Mama he practically ravaged her on the street. Charles didn't care, but he knew Rosslyn would.

Pulling back he watched as her eyes fluttered open. "I . . . um . . . we're . . ."

"We're going to be late for the fireworks if we don't get moving."

"You mean they haven't started?" Rosslyn teased.

Oh, don't tempt me, sweetheart. He smiled down at her, not answering. Instead he took her hand and headed toward the music again. It was hard to pull away. He didn't care if they blew off going to the commons and went to his place instead. But that would cause a lot of questions he wasn't ready to answer. *Like my last name.* He intentionally hadn't mentioned it. And oddly, she hadn't asked either. Did that mean she already knew?

Could Rosslyn actually be out with him trying to obtain information for Maxwell? Nothing would surprise him where Maxwell was concerned. And hell, he couldn't be pissed at Rosslyn if that actually was the case. He had planned on doing that exact thing at first. Somewhere along the way, he'd forgotten why he was with her. *Now I'm with her only because I want to be.*

As Mama had so nicely told Rosslyn, Charles had never brought a woman to that restaurant. It had always been his escape. A place where he could be Charlie instead of Charles, even though he hated that name. But when he'd asked her to lunch, there was no doubt as to where he wanted to take her. *Maybe Gareth is right. She's more of a distraction than I can afford right now.*

Once they rounded the bend and he saw her eyes light up, he knew he'd made the right choice. He guided her to his favorite spot for watching the fireworks. When he got there the trees were taller than he remembered, and the crowd a bit closer too. But there was room for the two of them, as though it had been saved.

As they sat on the grass and snuggled close, the sky lit up in a burst of colors and shapes, and he knew she was a distraction he couldn't go without.

As they watched, Rosslyn turned to him and said, "You really surprised me, Charles."

"Is that a good thing?" he asked.

"Most definitely. I really needed this tonight. Thank you so much."

He felt her relax against him as she rested her head on his

shoulder. *I think I needed this just as much.* "I'm glad you're enjoying yourself." He tightened his hold slightly and she snuggled closer. Charles had surprised himself tonight as well.

The fireworks were over and they sat quietly. He didn't want to move. Rosslyn's cell phone rang and, in a panic, she searched her purse and pulled it out quickly. "Dad, is everything okay?" Charles could feel as well as see her distress. He placed a hand on her back to let her know he was there. "Oh, that's good. I was worried. But I promise I'll call tomorrow morning. Maybe Mom will want to talk then. I love you, Dad." Then she ended the call.

That wasn't a normal response for a parent calling. Not at this age at least. "Is everything okay? Do you need to go?'

Rosslyn nodded. "I usually call my Dad every night. He was worried about me." With a sigh she added, "That's not entirely true. We speak every night because my mother is ill. All we have is each other to lean on when things are difficult."

That explained the sadness he's seen in her eyes. It had returned. "I'm here if you want to talk about it."

"Thanks. But you really don't want to hear about my—"

"I do. If it will help, that is." Charles meant it too.

"My mother has Parkinson's and is having more and more complications. My Dad said she had a bad day today, and I . . . I wish I could be there to help him."

"Do you want me to take you now?" Rosslyn looked at him as though he was joking. But he wasn't. "I'm serious. If you want we can leave right now."

"Thank you, Charles, but all he needed was to talk for a few minutes. Hopefully tomorrow will be a better day. Besides, I can't travel back and forth every weekend."

"Too far?"

"Too expensive. That's what I'm doing here in the city. I'm working to help pay my mother's medical bills."

God. And I thought you might be . . . Damn I'm such an asshole. "It sounds like it's not only hard on your father."

"I guess not. But I'd do just about anything to make it easier on them."

Here they sat—Rosslyn driven by doing good and Charles driven by revenge. Could they be any different? *Hell, this woman is too good for me.* That didn't mean he was cutting ties. If anything, with what he'd just learned, he needed to make sure she wasn't hurt in the crossfire. He somehow had to keep her out of it all. That plan was going to take some time, and some help, to coordinate.

"It sounds like you've had a big day. Why don't I take you home so you can get some rest?" He could tell she was mentally exhausted.

"I am kind of tired. Are you sure you don't mind?"

"Not at all." He got up and extended a hand to her. They were quiet as they walked back to his vehicle. He had no idea what she must be going through. Charles hated saying he was born with a silver spoon in his mouth, but in a way, it was the truth. He might have had a lot of challenges, but lack of money wasn't one of them. He really didn't know much about Parkinson's. That was going to change. If he was going to be there for her, he needed to know what she was facing. From what Rosslyn said, it didn't sound promising. There were only a few things money couldn't buy. But maybe he could help ease her burden.

If she'll even accept my help. Once she found out who he was, probably not.

When he pulled in front of her building he kept the engine running. Getting out and walking her inside was asking for this night to take a different direction. If it had been someone else, someone he wasn't so fond of, he'd go for it. But Rosslyn was the most genuinely sweet person he'd met in a long time. She wasn't chasing a grand dream wanting to live in the lap of luxury. What drove her came from the very core of everything that was good in this world. *Damn. There should be more people like her.*

Charles reached over and covered her hand with his. "Are you sure you're going to be okay?"

Rosslyn nodded. "Unfortunately there are things one can't change. I'll call my father first thing in the morning and hopefully my mother will be up to talk on the phone."

"Would it be okay for me to call and check on you?" Charles couldn't believe he asked that. Her eyes glistened, and he was afraid she'd burst out crying. He wasn't good at dealing with tears. Hell, he avoided them like the plague. And now he felt like shit for upsetting her. *Fuck.* "I'm sorry. I was only trying to be—"

"Nice." Rosslyn sniffed. "You have no idea how much that means to me."

Changing the subject, he said, "I don't know about you, but I'm all cheesecaked-out. I know a place that has the best wieners around. Do you like wieners?"

Rosslyn laughed and didn't let him off the hook. "Well *Charlie,* call me tomorrow, and I'll let you know. Now I better get upstairs before you deliver another horrendous pick-up line."

Charles laughed. "Oh, trust me, they get worse."

"Thanks for the warning."

Before she got out of the car, he leaned over and kissed her tenderly. Looking into her eyes he said, "If you need to talk, I'm only a call away."

"Same here." Then she got out of the car, and he waited until she was inside the secured building.

As he pulled away he couldn't help but laugh to himself. *Do you like wieners? Really classy.* But he loved the fact she picked up on the play on words and gave it right back. Maybe she wasn't as fragile as he thought. Which in this city was a good thing. Hell, working for Maxwell, it was a requirement.

But that employment is short-lived.

6

She couldn't sleep one bit. Between her father's phone call and her outing with Charles, she was on an emotional roller-coaster. Why did he have to be so freaking nice and under-standing about everything? He got it, she was here and alone and Charles cared. Max and Laura on the other hand, didn't even offer dinner, never mind a place to stay for free.

But she had judged New York City based on how they had treated her and her family. She was quickly learning that not all here were so self-absorbed. Actually she hadn't met anyone as cold as her so-called family. Maybe being in the city wasn't going to be as bad as she'd thought. Unfortunately her employer was the only downfall.

But today she didn't need to think about work. She'd already called her parents and had a better conversation than she'd had in a while. Miss Snuggles was fed, brushed, and petted, so she was all set for a few hours. Now all she had to do was wait to see when or if Charles was going to call. She didn't want to admit she'd never had a wiener before. Well not the kind he was referring to at least. A hot dog with meat, onions, and celery salt sounded like a weird combination. But it provided another reason to see him today, so she was game. If he called.

But times had changed. It was acceptable for a woman to call a man. Actually many women took the lead these days. She wasn't ready to go that far, but he did say call anytime. Looking at the clock, she figured it was almost noon, and he didn't strike her as the sleep late type of guy. Nervously she dialed his number. It rang once, twice, and then three times. What would she say if she got voice mail? *Hey, is your offer for a wiener still good?*

She panicked and hung up. Instead she decided to send him a text. Staring at her phone, she didn't want to put anything weird in writing any more than she did on his voice mail. *Something simple.*

She typed that she had a good time last night but deleted it. She told him that yesterday. She didn't want to thank him, that could easily be responded to with a "you're welcome." So she decided to search the internet for anything fun and free to do today. It was beautiful outside, and she didn't want to spend it looking out a window. *Perfect!*

GO FLY A KITE

She didn't need to wait long before her phone rang. It was Charles.

"I thought you had a good time yesterday," Charles said.

"I did."

"Then why did you tell me to go fly a kite?" he asked.

She looked back at her text. *Oh God.* "Sorry. My cell phone seems to have a mind of its own. What I meant to ask was if you *wanted* to go fly a kite." That really didn't sound any better, so she tried explaining. "There is a kite show that I thought might be . . . different."

God, he probably thinks it's stupid. But he had taken her to see fireworks last night. That was more in line with a romantic date. Kite flying really wasn't just for children. Not the type of kites they had shown online. Heck, they probably cost more than what she made in a week.

"Do you mean in Central Park?" Charles asked.

"Yes, but if you—"

"That sounds great. Do you have a kite?"

"No. Do you?"

He laughed. "I hate to admit it, but I've never flown one. I have been told I should many times."

He was teasing her now. That's okay. She earned that one. "Any issue with grabbing a blanket and we watch them instead?"

"Do you mind if I bring food?"

Rosslyn laughed and said teasingly, "I like a man who knows how to negotiate."

"I'm really good about calling ahead too. What do you feel like?" he asked.

Wieners off the table? "Something small because I'm still full from last night. You weren't kidding when you said the dishes were humongous."

"How about sandwiches?"

"How about I make some?" She didn't have much in the apartment, but she had enough to make a few sandwiches and two packs of chips.

"I don't want you to have to work."

"We're talking sandwiches. Meat and cheese between two slices of bread. That's not considered work."

"Okay, I'll call you when I'm close by."

"I'll be ready." She ended the call and headed to the kitchen to make sandwiches. She figured he was good for more than one the way she'd seen him eat. Placing sliced ham, turkey, and cheese on the counter, she started making the sandwiches when her cell phone rang in the other room. Placing the knife down, she rushed to answer it, thinking it was her father. But it was Liz instead. And she was crying.

"I can't believe it. Everything was perfect last night. Then . . . then he asked me to quit my job. That he couldn't stand the fact I worked for someone so . . . crooked."

Rosslyn could see both sides. For Sam, it was a constant reminder of how he'd been screwed over. But for Liz, it was her stability. Her independence. Sam had to know that wasn't easy for Liz to walk away from. But what did Rosslyn know about such things? She'd never been put in that situation. Would she choose a man over it all?

She didn't need to know how things like that could work out. Her mother had done exactly that. Walked away from a billion-dollar business and inheritance just to be with the man she loved. And from what Rosslyn could tell, her mother never regretted it either. But were they the exception to the rule? Would Liz and Sam survive, or would the struggles be too much for them? That wasn't anything Rosslyn could advise her on.

"It sounds like you have a lot of thinking to do."

"Really? You don't think he's asking too much?" Liz asked.

"I don't know. But we do things for people we love that we wouldn't do for anyone else."

"True."

"Did he say you had to answer him immediately?" Because no one liked an ultimatum. That's what happened to her mother. Her grandfather said, "Never speak to that man again, or never speak to me again." The rest was history. Her grandfather died and her mother wasn't even allowed to go to the funeral. It was surprising that Uncle Max still spoke to her. Obviously not in years, though, since Max didn't know her mother was ill. *What a fucked up family. I'm so glad I didn't grow up around them.*

"Sam told me to think about it. But I know he's not going to budge on this."

"It sounds like he really cares about you, Liz. So maybe if you make a list of everything you can't live without, then you'll know what you want to do." If Sam was on that list, Liz should tell Max to screw. Of course Max would hire someone else in the blink of an eye. He had loyalty only to one person. *Himself.*

"Thanks for listening to me, Rosslyn. I needed someone to tell me what I already knew. I can't make a snap decision. And if he really loves me, he'll understand that."

"Exactly, Liz. Are you okay now?"

"Yup. I'll see you Monday. Bright and early."

Oh yay. "Have a good weekend."

She ended the call and headed back to the kitchen. Rosslyn couldn't believe what she saw. Sweet Miss Snuggles had taken all the sliced meat and was eating it. Even the cheese was on the floor. Not only did she make a huge mess, but she ruined the only stuff Rosslyn had to make sandwiches.

She grabbed the meat from the cat, not sure how good that was going to be on her digestive system, and threw it all in the trash.

"You have no idea what you have done, do you? What is Charles going to think when we have nothing to eat?" If things weren't bad enough, she now was talking to a cat. Miss Snuggles didn't seemed troubled by Rosslyn's predicament in the least as she purred and rubbed against her legs.

Once the floor was clean, Rosslyn started looking through the refrigerator for an alternative. There was raspberry jelly. Then she grabbed the jar of peanut butter in the cupboard. *I can't believe this.* She promised him lunch. Good thing she wasn't specific, because PB&J and bottled water was it.

Her phone rang again and she turned to Miss Snuggles and said, "Don't you dare touch that bag." Then she went into the other room and answered. "Hi Charles, are you almost here?"

"I'll be there in five minutes."

"Great. See you then."

Slipping the phone in the back pocket of her jeans, she grabbed her keys and went to check on the bag. Miss Snuggles hadn't moved and everything seemed as she'd left it. Giving her a quick pat, she headed out the door.

It wasn't long before they were on their way for what seemed like one of the most unique dates she'd been on in a long time. Being with Charles made it special, at least for her. It didn't matter what they did, she enjoyed being with him. From what she could tell, he felt the same.

She pulled out the sandwiches and said, "Hope you don't have a peanut allergy."

"No allergies at all. Why?"

"I prepared gourmet raspberry jam, with creamy peanuts." Winking, she explained, "Peanut butter and jelly."

Charles took a bite. "Oh God. I haven't had one of these in years."

"There might be a good reason for that."

"I forgot how good they are. I hope you made me more than one."

"Okay, you can quit teasing me now."

He looked at her and realized she really didn't believe him. "Maybe if you take a bite, you'll realize I'm not joking."

"I eat them every morning."

"Then why did you decide on them for lunch?" he asked.

Rosslyn sighed. "It's not what I had planned, but the cat I'm watching thought the ham and turkey were for her."

"The cat ate them?" Rosslyn nodded. "I'm glad. I prefer these."

"Well they go along with the theme."

"So do chocolate covered bananas."

Her eyes widened. "I should've made those."

"What?"

"A peanut butter and banana sandwich," Rosslyn said.

"Next time."

She giggled. "Oh no. The pressure is on. How can I top these?"

"Guess we'll have to go out again to find out." Charles couldn't believe he was suggesting they keep this going.

"Only if you promise to do more of the talking. Right now you seem to know a lot more about me than I do you."

"What do you want to know?" Charles wasn't sure giving her that power was a good idea, but he'd answer honestly no matter what she asked.

"Tell me about your family."

"I have five younger brothers, all pretty much local, living either in the city or nearby. My father is retired, and he and my mother spend their time traveling."

"After raising six boys, I bet she needed a vacation."

He laughed. "A few of my brothers may have given her a few gray hairs. I, on the other hand, was a—"

"Don't bother saying angel. Mama told me a few stories about you and Salvatore."

"I'd never claim that. But when I was at home, I spent most of my time with my father. So whenever I got a break, I hung out with Sal. He showed me how to . . . have fun. Oddly enough my brothers never would believe the stories."

"Why is that?"

"Being the eldest, the responsibility to be a good role model fell on my shoulders. That meant not getting caught doing anything wrong."

"Ah, I get it. You had to *look* like the perfect child when in fact you were a little hellion."

"Hey, what did Mama tell you?" Charles had been concerned leaving the two alone while he went to the men's room during dinner.

"She made me promise not to tell."

"Is that how it is?"

Rosslyn shrugged. "She said if I did, there would be no more desserts for me. Since she's an amazing cook, there's no way I can rat her out."

"I might need to find a new place to take you. Someplace where no one knows me."

"Don't worry. They weren't that bad. Actually she said you were the one who kept Sal out of trouble most of the time."

"She was being kind." Actually that wasn't the case. Sal had a lot of time on his hands. He plotted and planned their misadventures right down to the excuse they were going to use if they got caught. They were some of the best childhood memories he had. *Because being with Sal was the only time I was allowed to be a child.*

"I'm jealous. Being an only child was tough. When something was wrong, my parents knew exactly who to blame."

Charles cocked a brow. "You'll never get me to believe you were a wild child."

"The wildest thing I ever did was skinny dip off the boat one night."

"Obviously, your stories are much more interesting than mine. Maybe we should go back to talking about you."

"Good try. We did that the last two times. Unless you want me to ask Mama?"

"No. That's okay. What else do you want to know?"

"Hmm. What do you do for a living?" Rosslyn asked.

That was heading where he didn't want to go. "I'm an architect by trade."

"Wow. That's exciting. I can't even build a house out of a deck of playing cards."

He laughed. "Neither can I. But I can play a mean game of poker."

She grinned and said, "I bet you can. Has anyone ever told you you're hard to read?"

"It's a good thing on the job."

"Maybe as a spy, but as an architect, I don't get it. Isn't everything laid out on paper anyway?" Rosslyn asked.

"I guess I do more than that. There is the other side filled with contracts and overseeing staff. It comes in handy then." Rosslyn seemed to be more in touch with who he was then he'd anticipated. He wasn't sure this was a good thing. She somehow was chiseling away at his walls.

"I never thought about that side of it. What made you want to be an architect?"

She meant it—today was going to be all about the life of Charles. He preferred it to be a closed book; only his family and very close friends knew anything real about him. She was inching her way into that fold very smoothly.

"It's a family business so I kind of fell into it." *Not that I had a choice back then.* He had no idea what he'd do if it wasn't that. Thankfully he liked what he did, at least most of it.

"I'm glad I didn't follow in my father's footsteps. I love being on the boats, but people would be in serious trouble if I was repairing them. I can't even change a flat tire. Of course, I don't own a car so that's not an issue either."

"You don't need one in the city, but even back home you don't have one?"

"No. I like to bike or walk. It's not that I can't drive. I have a license. Why pay for something you're not going to use?"

"I really could use someone who thinks like that on my staff. I have a few who believe you should have something just in case you might need it."

"That sounds ridiculous. But I don't know anything about your business. Heck. I don't know much about where I work either. I always thought a personal assistant did more. Guess it's just a fancy name for errand girl."

She finally was talking about Grayson Corp. Even though they were having a nice time, he had to ask. "How is it working for them?" *Maxwell specifically.*

"I've only been there a week. Actually the first time I saw you, I was discussing my position. That was Mr. Grayson, in case you didn't know."

Oh I fucking know. "He's well known."

"That's what I hear. I see Grayson Corp plastered all over the city. Guess I should consider myself lucky to be working there. It should look great on my resume."

Most people talked about growing with a company and working toward a promotion. She talked like she could be out of there any time. It was coming, but there was no way she knew anything about it. "Not planning on staying?"

She shook her head. "The way things are progressing with my mom, I won't need to."

Rosslyn didn't need to say the words. Why did he keep asking questions that brought her heartache? His paranoia was causing him to think she knew more than she was letting on. If anything, Rosslyn was the last person he needed to worry about. She had more important things to worry about than what happened to Maxwell Grayson. He's nothing to her but a paycheck. That's something she could get anywhere.

"Are you sure you don't want to take a drive up there today?"

She said, "If you haven't noticed, we're out at a park and supposed to be admiring the different kites."

"I've been looking. Dragons, Boxes. Fish. Hell, if I'm right, that one over there is a monkey. But if you want to be with your parents, that's where you should be." He knew she was torn and only needed a little push.

"The bus has already left and there isn't another until tomorrow. I wouldn't make it back in time for work on Monday if I go. Getting fired won't be helping them." She sighed. "Sometimes it sucks doing what is right instead of what you want to do."

Don't I know it. "What if we drove?"

"We?"

"I've got nothing planned for the weekend."

"And you want to drive six hours to Alexandria Bay? Why?"

"So you can visit your parents," Charles said.

"That's not very exciting for you. My mother has dementia. She might not even know you're there. Or worst, she might not like you."

"I don't know. I can be pretty charming when I try." Charles gave her a dashing smile. Then he got serious. "And this isn't about whether she likes me or not. It's so you can see her."

"I still have no idea what's in it for you."

He gave her a playful wink. "If it's still warm tomorrow,

maybe you can show me that swimming hole you like to skinny dip in."

She blushed and said, "I am so going to regret telling you that."

Charles tapped her on the tip of her nose. "Most definitely. Now what do you say? Pack up and head to Alexandria Bay?"

"I need to stop at the apartment first and make sure the cat has plenty of food and water. The owners would flip out if anything happened to her while they were gone."

"Not your cat?"

"Not my place. I'm house-sitting and the house comes with a cat. Three more weeks and they'll be back."

"Then let's get going." The sandwiches were gone so packing up was easy—trash and a blanket. He couldn't stop thinking about her current living arrangement. Three weeks wasn't a long time. And finding someplace else in New York took time. *What will happen then?* He wasn't sure she'd still have a job at that point. Once he had everything he needed, Charles was going to the Feds. He couldn't let how this would affect Rosslyn get in his way. Not at this point. *Not at all.*

It was probably easier thought than done. He was going with her to see her family, and she hadn't even invited him. Hell, he invited himself. Charles was losing his focus. Yet he wasn't backing out. Alexandria Bay was a part of her, a place that helped mold her into who she was. Charles really wanted to see her in her own environment. Maybe that would break whatever spell she had on him. *Or finish me off.*

Guess it didn't matter because after one quick stop, they were on their way.

As Rosslyn was upstairs checking on the cat, Charles

figured he'd touch base with Gareth one more time. "Anything new on Maxwell?"

"Not sure. Hell Charles, I'm not sure what to make of this."

He wasn't used to hearing Gareth puzzled. Usually his cocky self was bragging about how easy everything was. "Maybe I can help."

Gareth laughed. "You stick to what you do, let me handle this."

"Then at least let me know what has the great Gareth stumped, so I can enjoy your struggles."

"You know you can be an ass sometimes, right?" Gareth growled.

Charles laughed. "It's the small things in life that we enjoy the most. Now, are you going to tell me or not?"

"Someone was doing some digging into our family."

That caught Charles's full attention. "All of us? One of us?"

"See that's what is strange. Not us. But our grandfather."

That made no sense. He'd died about ten years ago. "Are you sure about that?"

"I'm telling you, his name had been searched. Did you know dad had a sister?" Gareth asked.

"No, he never mentioned it. What happened?"

"Guess she went missing when she was a young girl. They never found her. Dad was really young then, so maybe he didn't remember her."

But their grandfather would've. How come no stories, no pictures of her? Losing a daughter might explain why their grandfather was so abusive to their father. He must've been filled with anger and didn't know how to deal with it. Of course taking it out on your only living child was stupid.

"Was it Maxwell or his people doing the digging?"

"No. Some woman from a small town in Rhode Island. No connections to anyone. Not even to New York. That's why it makes no sense at all. But she does work for a very well-known family, the Hendersons, in Boston."

Charles had heard of them. Although he'd never actually done any business with them, they had been one of his first solo assignments. God, that was years ago. Charles had been working under his father at that time, and like Dylan, he was out to prove himself. Lawson Steel even bid on the development of one of their new buildings. He couldn't remember all the details, but it was in some foreign country. The place had been unstable but Charles wanted that contract. Just like he had done to Dylan, their grandfather had done to him. No explanation. He just told them Lawson Steel was not to do any business with the Hendersons. At that time, he was pissed. He'd been so close to signing his first contract with one hell of a powerful family.

Even if the Hendersons found out that his grandfather had blocked the contract, they wouldn't care. From what he heard, Brice Henderson and Asher Barrington went ahead and built their facility anyway. All this was old news. There had to be something else. And if it involved their grandfather, it could be just about anything.

"Let's not say anything to anyone," Charles stated.

"I was thinking about asking Dad," Gareth replied.

"No. Just see if you can find out anything. Even if you need to reach out to the woman directly. It's probably nothing."

"If you think that, you don't know the Hendersons' reputation. You don't get that powerful without some skeletons in your closet."

Charles said, "That would go for the Lawson family as well."

"Do you know something I don't?"

Of course. "Just that our grandfather wasn't a saint. It wouldn't surprise me if he'd gone head to head with them years ago." He hoped that's all it was. Charles had enough with Grayson to deal with. He didn't need to start a list of Lawson enemies.

"I might have a few myself," Gareth laughed. "You're probably the only one who lives such a boring ass life, working all the time."

"I'm taking the weekend off. That's why I'm calling. I'll check back in on Monday."

"Should I assume it has something to do with R. Clark?"

"Don't assume anything and don't waste your breath asking either. I'll talk to you Monday." He ended the call just as Rosslyn was leaving the building. He wasn't sure what to expect regarding her mother's health. He'd never realized until now that he'd never visited anyone who was sick. *Seems like there's going to be a lot of firsts with Miss Rosslyn Clark.*

7

Her heart was pounding and not just because Charles was sitting beside her. What was she thinking, letting him come home with her? This was no time to play "meet my parents." Her father had his hands full keeping things as normal as possible. Unfortunately, that changed from day to day.

"You're awfully quiet," Charles said.

"Thinking." *that this is a mistake.*

"Worried about your mother?"

"Every moment. You can just drop me off if you don't want to come inside."

"It's not an issue for me. The question is, is it for you?" Charles asked as they turned onto her street.

She wasn't about to lie to him. "It's been a long time since I brought someone home with me. It's possible they get the wrong impression."

"Just tell them that I care about you and knew this was where you wanted . . . no needed, to be this weekend. Very simple."

Internally she laughed. *Nothing about you is simple.* "I wasn't thinking. No one knows you're coming. Heck, they don't know I'm coming. Things can be . . . complicated at night. I'm thinking this was a bad idea."

"Mornings are better for your mother?" Charles asked.

"Yes. Which would make the visit more enjoyable for you." Not that it was going to be good either way, but once her mother started to "sundown" things became unpredictable. *And it'd be nice if she knew my name too.*

"Rosslyn, I meant what I said. I'm okay with whatever you want."

"Tomorrow morning would be best."

"Let me book us a hotel room and then we can have dinner. How does that sound?" Charles asked.

It seemed so weird being in her hometown and staying at a hotel. "I know a friend who runs a B&B. She will probably give you a great deal." *Not that you're worried about money. But I am.*

"Sounds good."

Rosslyn sent a quick text to her friend Brandy. Who would've thought she was busy this weekend, but she said she'd squeeze them in. Turning her attention back to Charles, she said, "We're all set. You're going to love this place. It's a huge old Victorian with a wraparound porch."

"Point the way."

It wasn't all that far from where they were. When they pulled up she felt totally relaxed. And as soon as she got out of the car, she knew why. It was quiet. That was something she didn't have in the city. Letting out a long exhale she said, "This is nice."

"Being home?" he asked.

"That too. But being here where we can hear ourselves think."

"It's been a while since I've had a weekend that wasn't filled with work."

"If your boss doesn't give you time off, you need to work for someone else." She didn't understand why he had a smirk on his face. She was totally serious. "I'm serious. I hear people complaining all the time about their working conditions, long hours, no breaks and no appreciation. The only thing Max—Mr. Grayson—wants is results. They stay for the money, but there are so many more important things in life than money."

"You are working for him."

"I explained why. If it was for me, I wouldn't be in the city, never mind working for someone like him."

"And if you had the option, what would you do?" Charles asked.

She chuckled. "I'd strip down and jump in the lake, without a care in the world." Rosslyn saw his eyes widen and she said, "Not serious. Please, I skinny dipped one time and that was many years ago. There is no way in hell it's ever happening again."

Charles laughed. "Not that I wouldn't mind seeing you take that dip"—he winked—"but I meant if you had the option for another *job*."

Rosslyn blushed. "Oh. I thought you were . . . never mind." Why did she think for a second that he was going to offer her a job just to see her naked? Then again, she didn't know why she had mentioned it in the first place. *Maybe because I hoped you offer to join me.* He really was awakening something more . . . playful in her. A side she'd thought was dead. It was nice and refreshing. But it was not the time for that.

To answer his question, she thought about what she'd do if presented with such an option. Most people would jump at the chance, but she couldn't. "If someone offered me a job starting immediately, I'd have to say no. Even though

Grayson Corp isn't my dream job, I would need to give at least two weeks' notice." She tried to live her life by treating people how she'd want to be treated. Rosslyn tried not to put down others, but she knew her aunt and uncle weren't role models of kindness and compassion.

"Do you think Maxwell would give you two weeks' notice if he was going to fire you?"

She knew he wouldn't. If she had doubted that, listening to what he'd done to Sam and his brother confirmed Max never thought how his actions affected anyone else. *If he had, he'd have stood by his sister. Or at least reconnected after their father died. But no. He still pretends the Clarks aren't his family. We barely exist to him.*

Rosslyn realized Charles had somehow turned the tables and she was the focus of the conversation. *Good try.* "I believe it's your career we were discussing, not mine."

"My boss is a hard-ass. Expects only the best from me and won't settle for anything less."

"He sounds horrible. You need to explain to him that no one is perfect and if you push too hard, you can break someone. I can't say for sure, but you seem to be responsible and are probably a very good employee."

"We all have our moments." Charles laughed.

Once again, Rosslyn didn't know what he found so funny. No one wanted to be miserable at work. Unfortunately many people had no choice. "I guess you need to do what you have to in order to pay the bills. Just like the rest of us."

Charles looked like he wanted to say something, staring at her intently, but then turned away. "I don't know about you, but that porch looks tempting. Why don't we check into our rooms then occupy that swing for a while?"

"Sounds great."

When they got inside Brandy was there to greet them.

"Well now I know why you didn't want to spend the night at home with your parents. I'm Brandy and you are?"

"Charles."

"Where are you from Charles?" she asked.

"New York City."

"Did you two need help with your bags?" Brandy asked.

Rosslyn shot Charles a quick look and said, "We didn't pack anything."

"We can buy anything we need tomorrow if you have extra toiletries."

"That I have. Come, I'll show you to your room."

They followed her upstairs to one of the largest rooms she had. It had a four poster bed and embroidered duvet cover. The entire room was filled with antiques, including the wicker rocker by the window. It had always been Rosslyn's favorite room, but she'd never had a reason to stay there. Why would she when she lived only ten minutes away?

Brandy said, "The washroom is through that door and you'll find what you need in the cabinet. Breakfast is at nine, but coffee is one hour earlier. Please let me know if either of you need anything else before then."

Brandy was about to close the door when Rosslyn asked, "What about my room?"

"There's just the one," Brandy said.

"You don't have another one?"

Brandy shook her head. "You're lucky I had a last minute cancelation because everything in town is booked. They are having a fishing tournament this weekend. Enjoy your night."

When the door closed, Rosslyn turned to Charles and said, "I had no idea."

"I'm sure you didn't. Do you have an issue with sharing a room with me?"

Her heart skipped a few beats. *Issue. No. Concern? Yes.* "Not . . . really. It's just a bit . . . unexpected, that's all."

"I'd say that sums up just about everything about you," Charles said.

"I'm not sure that's a compliment."

Charles walked over and tipped her chin up so she couldn't avoid looking him in the eyes. "Trust me Rosslyn, it is. I find myself trying to guess what's next. And not once have I been right." She felt as though she couldn't breathe. Wanting to look away, yet not able to break the connection. He was drawing her to him with just his eyes. He continued, "But there's always a first time."

Charles leaned over and kissed her gently then pulled away, still looking down at her. "That was . . . nice, but—"

"But not enough?" Charles asked.

Rosslyn knew she shouldn't be doing this, but she wanted him. Was it so wrong to have a little bit of joy in her life? From the way her body was warming and the tingling between her legs, she didn't want to deny herself. Let them have tonight. Tomorrow's reality would come soon enough. She shook her head. "Not even close."

Charles gave her a wicked grin. "Like I said, you're always a surprise."

I think I'm surprising myself too.

She reached her arms up and wrapped them around his neck, encouraging him to kiss her again. A moan escaped her as he claimed her lips with such passion it ignited a fire within her. He traced her lips with his tongue, asking her to let him in, and she parted them. His tongue swept through her mouth briefly, a tease, and then pulled back so only the tips of their tongues danced with each other before exploring again. *Damn, this man can kiss.*

Over and over, he kissed her, until they were both gasping for breath. "Better?" Charles asked.

"Getting closer," she challenged.

"Don't tempt me to make it so neither of us can remember our names."

She licked her lips, "I'd love to see that."

Charles loosened his grip so her feet once again touched the floor. She hadn't realized he'd lifted her up, that's how sweet his kisses were. He kissed his way down her neck, causing a shiver to run through her as his beard tickled in such a fun erotic way.

She could feel her breasts swell and her nipples harden, aching for attention. Rosslyn arched her back to draw his attention to them. He looked up at her and all she could see was his eyes, now so dark they reflected her need in them. *God, I could get lost forever looking into those eyes.*

"Charles, I . . . I . . ."

"Oh, you still know my name. I'm going to have to work harder," he teased as he nipped her earlobe.

She moaned and was once again at a loss for words. His hand rested just below her breasts. "Maybe we should let our bodies do the talking."

"Then let me begin this conversation." His hand moved over her hip and across her stomach. His fingers slowly inched lower, yet he never broke eye contact with her.

Oh . . . that feels so good. His hands continued to caress her through her clothes and it felt so damn good already. She wanted to feel more of his sweet touch.

She couldn't wait any longer. Her hands began doing some exploring of their own. She reached out and tugged his T-shirt out of his jeans then tried to pull it over his head. He was so much taller than she was, but he assisted and tossed it on the floor. Now, Rosslyn had a clear view of his bare chest, and his huge biceps. *Perfection.*

Running her hands up his arms, she felt him tense with her touch.

"I—"

"Shh. Just feel." His voice was deeper and huskier.

She wasn't sure if it was desire or raw passion that was overtaking her, but all inhibitions were cast aside. Rosslyn had never wanted anyone like she did him. If she could've ripped the clothes from his body and pushed him on the bed, she would've. The fire burning inside her was intense, and she wanted—no, she *needed*—to have more.

Her hands moved across his muscular chest, then down over his abs, only to grip the bottom of his T-shirt and pull it over his head. She wanted to rake her hands over every inch of him, but he was still overdressed. She reached for the button on his jeans, flipped it open, and moved to the zipper. Once free, she slipped her right hand inside and felt him harden at her touch.

"Fuck," he groaned.

"Shh. Just feel," she said to him this time.

Charles grabbed her wrists and pulled them away. She sucked in her breath, hoping he wasn't about to stop, not now.

"Please, Charles I—"

"I know, sweetheart, but you first."

He lifted her T-shirt over her head, then unbuttoned her shorts and slid them over her hips. Although she loved the feel of his fingers brushing against her bare skin, and she enjoyed each and every touch, the ache between her legs became almost unbearable. She *needed* him to touch her more intimately.

Rosslyn wished she'd worn some really sexy lingerie,

but none of this was planned. She'd planned a day flying kites at the park. Now it was her passion that was soaring higher than the clouds. She wanted no barriers between them, so she reached behind her back and unhooked her bra, letting it slip from her shoulders. Before she could slip out of her panties, Charles's hands were already sliding them down.

"Yes.. . . ." It was more of a sigh than a word.

Standing naked in front of him, she felt his eyes roaming all over her. Her insecurities were about to kick in when he mumbled, "You're so beautiful."

Charles stripped off the remainder of his own clothes before lifting her in his arms, carried her over to the bed, and laid her down before lying beside her. He ran a hand from her cheek, over her collarbone, then across her breast and lower. His hand crossed her abdomen, and when he passed her belly-button, his eyes followed the path his fingers were taking.

She opened her legs to him and closed her eyes as his fingers slipped through her wet folds and over her swollen clit. A shudder rippled through her. *Oh damn.*

Although Rosslyn hadn't had many lovers, Charles wasn't her first. But her body was reacting as though he knew every-thing she wanted, even before she did, like old lovers coming home.

It was sweet torture each time a finger slid over her clit. Her pulse was racing; this wasn't the time to be timid. Lifting her hips, she pumped her flesh against his hand.

She wanted him to replace his hand with his mouth, but she also wanted to please him. Rosslyn reached out and gripped his shoulders, practically digging into the taut muscles as she strained to open her legs wider.

"Yes, sweetheart." He increased the strokes over her clit, slipping a finger inside of her, sending waves of heat rushing through her veins, each stroke faster than the one before. The heat in the pit of her stomach spread throughout her body.

"Oh, Charles," she cried, "I need you, all of you."

"You'll have me, Rosslyn. After you give me what I want."

"But . . . I . . ." She moaned as he entered her again.

"I want to feel you quiver and lose control."

As he stroked her feverishly, Rosslyn's body went rigid, and her cries of passion echoed through the room as her core clenched around Charles's finger. *Sweet heaven.* Her body shook and her desire burned out of control as the first orgasm rippled through her. When she thought it would end, Charles entered her with a second finger, bringing her climax to yet another level. *Charles. Oh . . . God . . . Charles.* She swore her body lifted off the bed and she felt as though she couldn't breathe, yet didn't care.

Left panting with every cell of her body tingling, she tried to hold him but Charles slipped from the bed. She couldn't open her eyes but heard the sound of a foil packet being torn. When he returned, he settled himself between her legs. She ran her hand down his broad chest, over his rock-hard abs, and stopped at his cock. Wrapping her fingers around him, she slowly stroked him, long strokes from the base to the tip.

"If you don't stop, I won't be able to either."

Although she wanted to make him lose himself, she wanted it to be inside of her. Reluctantly, she released him. Knowing he wanted her as much as she wanted him made her burn even hotter with desire.

God, I want this man.

As she opened her mouth to tell him, he claimed her lips. His kiss, though rough, was met just as fiercely by her own. She was filled with such hunger, as though she couldn't get enough of him.

Charles looked deeply into her eyes, and she felt he could read every thought and see right into her soul. Her desire was reflected by his.

She felt the head of his cock between her wet folds, her juices ready to blend with his. He slowly entered her until he was completely inside her. *Yes . . . oh yes . . .*

He was so gentle, yet he was larger than anyone she'd been with, and it took time to adjust. It was the sweetest pain she'd ever known. But she needed more. She lifted her hips to him, begging him to give her more, and he did.

He plunged deep inside. "Oh, sweetheart, you feel so damn good."

She loved him calling her sweetheart and wasn't going to remind him they were showing, not telling. Rosslyn wanted the words. Maybe he needed them too.

He'd repositioned himself slightly, and each movement stroked her G-spot. *Never has it been this good.* Her moans filled the air. *So, so good.* What he was doing to her caused her body to shiver and tingle with newfound bursts of ecstasy. As the waves of another release flooded through her, she felt her toes curl with delight. "Charles, oh, Charles. Yes. Yes! Charles, yes!" she screamed and panted out, over and over again.

Then she felt his body tense like her own, and a deep growl escaped him as his own hot release joined hers. "Fuck. Oh . . . yes!" Charles growled out before collapsing beside her.

They both lay gasping for breath. Her entire body tingled from the multiple, mind-blowing orgasms he'd given her. She curled up against him. Her body was spent, yet she'd never felt better. Rosslyn wasn't sure what they'd experienced, but it wasn't just sex. It was as though every laugh, thought, and connection they'd shared had poured out through their bodies.

Charles stroked her arm gently and said, "That was . . ."

"Unexpected?" Rosslyn added.

"And then some. Will you be disappointed if I change my mind?"

"About what?" she responded nervously.

"The swing."

She had no idea what he was talking about. Rolling onto her elbow she looked down at him. "What are you talking about?"

"I promised you a nice night out on the porch."

Rosslyn rolled her eyes. "Oh Charlie, you more than held up your promise; we just changed the location."

He shook his head. "Damn it."

"What now?" she asked.

Laughing, "You still know my name. I'm going to have to fix that. Unless you have any objections."

"Charlie. Charlie. Charlie," she said teasingly.

8

Morning wasn't awkward in the least. That was odd because Charles never hung around long enough to wake entangled with his lover. Then again, there was a good reason for that. Once the sex was over, there was nothing left. That's not at all how he felt with Rosslyn.

Not that he was looking forward to meeting her parents, but he was excited to be spending the day with her.

When she came out of the washroom, she looked refreshed. "That was fast."

"Only because I wouldn't let you shower with me. Otherwise we'd never get downstairs for breakfast."

"Eating is overrated," Charles said.

"You say that now. Wait till you taste her homemade sticky buns."

Nothing is going to taste as good as you. "Then I better shower and get dressed."

"I'm going to call my parents and let them know we'll be stopping by shortly, if that is okay."

"Sounds good," Charles said as he headed into the washroom to take a quick shower.

There was a lot on his mind that hadn't been there before. When he'd suggested this trip, never had he envisioned how it would unfold.

He hadn't been concerned about meeting her parents. He was a friend who'd given her a ride, that's all. Or at least that's all it had been. Now he was the guy who'd ridden their daughter all night long, making her cry out his name over and over again.

It wouldn't be so bad, but hell, she looked well-loved too. She almost glowed. A guy could hide it, but Rosslyn's demeanor almost screamed it. Charles couldn't tell her not to look so happy. Actually he loved that look in her eyes. He'd fulfilled his promise and both were spent and couldn't think after round three. If it wasn't for exhaustion, there might have been round four.

As he dressed he could hear his cell phone ringing in the bedroom. He wasn't in the mood to talk to anyone this morning. He was trying to stay focused on not saying anything stupid to her parents. But whoever was calling really wanted to get in touch with him.

There was a knock on the door and Rosslyn said, "Do you want your phone?"

Not really. "Sure." He opened the door with just a towel wrapped around his waist. She looked at him with hunger in her eyes as she handed it to him.

"You better shut that door or I might have to call my parents back," Rosslyn said.

He chuckled and did as she suggested. Looking at the caller ID he saw it was Gareth. Charles didn't want to return his call, but for Gareth to keep ringing his phone, it had to be important.

Dialing the number, he was ready to remind him he

wasn't working this weekend. Gareth didn't give him a chance.

"What the fuck, Charles. I've called three times."

"I was in the shower," Charles said flatly. Not that he wanted there to be something wrong, but there better be something urgent.

"Well I have something to tell you that might just blow your fucking mind."

He couldn't imagine what was so important about Maxwell that it couldn't wait. But since they were already on the phone, he might as well hear Gareth out. He turned down the phone just in case. The last thing he wanted was for Rosslyn to hear Maxwell's name. Although things were good between them, he knew she wouldn't be happy to learn he was out to take down her employer.

"Can't it wait till Monday?"

"No," Gareth said firmly. "Actually, I don't know where you are, but you might want to get your ass back to New York."

No matter what Gareth had uncovered, it was only going to add to the already long list. Any one of those things was enough; together, they ensured Maxwell was done for good. So why the hell was Gareth acting as though this was the one they needed. *Probably because I've been pushing his ass to dot the i's and cross the t's.* Figures that the one brother he thought was the screw-off was the one keeping Charles in line, or at least trying.

"I told you, consider me off the grid. This also isn't the ideal time to talk business."

"Not alone?" Gareth asked.

"No."

"Dammit, Charles. Why the hell did you take my advice

now and decide to get a fucking life. This is important. Like major important."

"And it can't wait till tomorrow morning?"

"It's waited this long, so I guess twenty-four hours won't change anything. But I'm telling you, first thing in the morning, we meet. Got it?"

If Charles wasn't so irritated, he'd have laughed. Since when did Gareth start barking orders? "I'll call you in the morning. Now if you don't mind, I'm getting back to—"

"Rosslyn?"

"My day off." Gareth knew who Charles was with. He didn't need to voice it.

When he ended the call and walked out of the washroom, Rosslyn was sitting on the bed. She no longer looked as happy as she had before. He walked over and sat down beside her. She'd talk when she was ready, this much he knew.

"I can't believe it. Liz, a girl I've been talking to at work, was just fired."

"Why?" Charles asked.

"Max, Mr. Grayson, said he didn't like the company she was keeping. So he fired her."

"That's not uncommon with employers. They have a reputation to uphold. Was she associating herself with someone doing something illegal?"

"No. Actually the opposite. I just feel horrible for her. And now I'm worried about my job too."

"Why?"

She turned and looked at him. "Mr. Grayson told me never to speak to you. I don't know why. If he learns that we . . . well, that we *talked* he's going to be so pissed he'll fire me too."

Good. I hate you working for that bastard. That's not what she wanted to hear. So he tried going in another direction. "You know it's coming. All you need to do is prepare for that day. From the sounds of it, Liz wasn't."

"No. And if I show up Monday and he fires me, what do I do? My parents are counting on me."

He wanted to tell her he'd hired her. But he had a very strict policy. No one at Lawson Steel was allowed to be intimately involved. Friends? Yes. Sex? Hell no. It opened up something he didn't want to deal with as an employer. Since he was the CEO, he couldn't be the one to break that rule. *So hiring her is now out of the question. Way to go, Charles.* Offering her money probably wasn't going to go over well either. "I'm sure it he fires you, you'll think of something. You don't strike me as the type of woman who'll take a wrongful termination lying down."

Rosslyn laughed. "My *lying* down with you might be what gets me fired." She elbowed him in the side and said softly, "But well worth it."

"I'm glad you enjoyed it as much as I did."

She shook her head. "I don't know if I want breakfast anymore."

"Do you want a repeat?"

Rosslyn said, "That's not why. I just remembered that we may have . . . been a bit—"

"Loud?" Charles finished. She nodded. "I'm sure we woke a few people in the house."

She blushed. "Maybe the neighborhood. You forget, I live here."

Charles put an arm around her shoulder and said, "Great. So your parents will already know my name."

Rosslyn covered her face with her hands. "Oh God. I never thought of that. What are they going to think?"

"Probably that you're not totally miserable in the city."

She shot him a look. "You're really no help at all, are you?"

He shook his head. "Apparently not. Now let's get downstairs for breakfast. You promised me sticky buns and I'm holding you to it."

Rosslyn leaned over, kissed him quickly on the cheek, and said, "Then get your butt dressed because those cute *buns* of yours are not on the menu."

He kissed the top of her head and headed back into the washroom to dress. He loved her playfulness, even when things were stressful for her. Would she still feel that way when things finally blew up? There was no doubt Maxwell was chomping at the bit. He must suspect something, or someone. It was only a matter of time before he looked at Rosslyn. What Charles didn't understand was why Maxwell had singled him out? From what Rosslyn said, it wasn't as though all the Lawsons were off limits, just him. *You know I'm coming for you, don't you Maxwell? That's okay. Because I'm ready for the fight.*

It wasn't as bad as she had thought. Her mother knew who she was right away. That was the perfect way to be greeted. "Mom, I want you to meet my friend Charles."

Charles shook her hand. "Nice to meet you, Mrs. Clark."

Her mother didn't speak, but at least she smiled at Charles. Her father pushed the wheelchair from the kitchen to the living room. "Charles, why don't you come sit in here with us so we can get to know you."

"Dad, he's not here for the third degree. He was just nice enough to bring me up here for the day."

He shot her a look, and she watched as he turned back to

Charles. "The day? That's odd because I got a call late last night saying my daughter was in town."

Rosslyn was going to intervene, but Charles replied first. "We didn't want to disturb you so late knowing your . . . situation here."

Her father stared at Charles as though he wasn't so sure about that response. Then finally he said, "The important thing is our little girl is here now."

Rosslyn couldn't take her eyes off her mother. How had the shaking gotten so much worse in just a week? It had to be her imagination. Dad surely would've called her if something had changed. Then she remembered he had, but she hadn't picked up on it. At that time, she'd been distracted with Charles. She couldn't let that continue to happen. Her father needed her to be responsive to what he needed. *I'm his backup for when he needs to talk or needs a break. And what was I doing? Rattling the windows at the B&B all night. Really nice, Rosslyn. Way to win the daughter of the year with that one.*

"Do you work for Max?" her father asked.

Was it her imagination or did she just see Charles clench his jaw before answering?

"No sir, I work for Lawson Steel."

"Ha. Lawson is that bastard's competition. This really must piss Max off."

"Dad, he doesn't know, and I would like to keep it that way," Rosslyn said. "If he finds out, I could be fired."

"Let him fire you. Then you can come home where you belong instead of—"

"Please, Dad. We can talk about this some other time. I only have a few hours before we have to head back to the city." She didn't want to have this conversation in front of

Charles. He didn't know she was Maxwell's niece, and if her father kept talking, it was bound to slip out.

"You're right. Let's enjoy your visit. You can call me tomorrow night."

And then I'll have to answer all the questions I'm avoiding now. It beat the hell out of having Charles witness them.

The next few hours were spent talking about stories of her as a young girl. It was what her mother seemed to remember the most. They even pulled out a photo album, making Rosslyn want to crawl under the couch. Big hair was an understatement. It had been wild and her choice of clothes had matched.

On their drive back to the city, Charles said, "That was . . . very informative." He couldn't hide his amusement either, and she shot him a warning look. "Don't worry. I'm sure my family has a few photos of me I wish didn't exist.

"The question is when will I get to see them?" Rosslyn asked.

He laughed. "Never, if I get my hands on them first."

"That doesn't sound fair at all."

Charles shrugged. "I didn't twist your father's arm to bring them out."

"I don't know about that. I leave you guys alone for five minutes to get my mother some tea and I return to a room filled with laughter."

"You have to admit, your hair looks much better now than back then."

"I don't know. I was thinking about growing this out and maybe trying that style again. What do you think?"

"I'm not sure it would fit in my car. At least not without obstructing my view," Charles teased. Then he reached over and covered her hand with his. His teasing tone vanished as he said, "I'm glad you allowed me to tag along. It's obvious you're their pride and joy."

"Since I'm their only child, what choice do they have?" Rosslyn joked.

"I'm serious, Rosslyn. Your father told me all the sacrifices you've made so he could be home taking care of your mother. He might call you his little girl, but you've impressed him with the woman you've become."

She blushed hearing Charles talk about her like that. Rosslyn did what she had to, what was needed. She didn't want any praise. There was only one thing she wanted, and unfortunately it wasn't possible. *For my mother to make a full recovery.*

"That's what family does. When someone needs help, you help."

"You make it sound like that's the way all families work."

Rosslyn shrugged. "One could dream." She wasn't sure she was doing everything she could, but she was trying.

She yawned and Charles said, "Why don't you sleep? It's a long ride and you look exhausted."

"You didn't get any more sleep than I did."

"But you have more on your mind than I do. Now close your eyes. If I get tired, I'll pull over and sleep awhile."

She yawned again and wanted to argue with him. "Only if you promise never to mention those photos again."

Charles laughed. "You have my word. Now sleep, sweetheart."

Her eyes burned and even if she wanted to stay awake, she wasn't going to be able to. Leaning back in the seat, she let herself drift off, thinking it would be just for a few minutes. But she opened her eyes to the bright lights of the city.

"Charles, you were supposed to wake me," Rosslyn said.

He said, "That's okay. Listening to you talk in your sleep was a lot more fun."

Her eyes widened and she sat straight up. "I didn't, did I?"

"Yes. I would like to think you were dreaming of me. At least I hope so. It sounded a bit like it did last night."

Rosslyn blushed, laid back in the seat, and said, "I'm not sure if you're joking, but I choose to believe you're only teasing me." *Please be joking.* As they pulled up in front of her building she turned to him and said, "Thank you, Charles. This weekend was exactly what I needed."

"Me too. I'll give you a call tomorrow after work."

"Here's hoping I have a job in the morning," Rosslyn laughed. "But if not, I hope he fires me before I get out of bed. I wouldn't mind sleeping late tomorrow."

"Trust me, Rosslyn, he's not firing you. At least not tomorrow." He leaned over and kissed her. "Good night. Sweet dreams."

As she got out of the car and headed upstairs, she knew sweet were the only dreams she could have. Their time together was all she saw every time she closed her eyes. *And that wasn't a dream either.*

9

Rosslyn dragged herself into the office, knowing there was going to be a lot of chatter about Liz's termination. She wanted to tell them the truth behind it, but that would put her head on the chopping block. She wasn't sure if Uncle Max suspected she knew or not. Just because they worked in the same office didn't mean they'd become each other's confidant.

But somehow that was exactly what she had become to Liz. It must've been very difficult working so close with Max and not having anyone to vent to after she and Sam broke up. With Rosslyn coming in from out of town, Liz probably assumed she didn't know anyone. Lucky for Liz, Rosslyn wasn't fond of Max and Laura either. Although she'd prefer not having any other reason to dislike them than what she'd already had. All negativity did was suck the life out of a person.

This weekend was exactly what she'd needed to recharge her batteries. Of course no batteries were needed with Charles. The connection between them was . . . amazing, yet scary. She didn't want it to end. Now back in the city, she was afraid it would. Being here was like throwing ice water on yourself.

"Rosslyn, come in my office," Max barked on the intercom.

And here we go. She rushed to his office, but even if she ran, it never would be fast enough for him. Forcing a smile, Rosslyn said, "Good morning, Mr. Grayson. How was your weekend?"

"I didn't call you in here for small talk. Liz is gone. There will be a woman arriving from the temp agency within the hour. I want you to show her around. Understood?"

"Yes, Mr. Grayson. Anything else?"

"Laura and I will be traveling this week. Just because I'm not here to watch you, doesn't mean you can screw off."

"I wouldn't dream of it." In a normal situation, she would wish the them safe travels or ask where they were going. Nothing normal there. Anything she said wouldn't be accepted as the kind gesture it was meant to be. She'd probably be accused of prying into his personal life. *And I don't want to know anything about that.* "Is that all?"

"No. I want to confirm that *no one* is aware of our . . . connection."

"I haven't said a word."

"Good. You're not as daft as I thought."

Gee, thanks. But you're an even bigger asshole than I thought. Almost chocking on her forced smile, Rosslyn asked, "Would you like me to bring your coffee in now?"

"You should've done that when you came in this time."

Biting her lip she said, "I'm sorry. I'll get it right away." As she scurried off to make it, she thought to herself, *How is it no one has poisoned him yet?* She shuddered at the thought. Usually she was kind and understanding, but he was really pushing it. Was this all a test to see how much she'd take?

Rosslyn wasn't sure what Max's problem was. When her grandfather died, everything was left to him, the business and the money. He had everything he wanted at his fingertips and, from what she could tell, he had his health as well. What he needed was a good old-fashioned butt-whooping to straighten him out. Maybe then he'd be a bit more . . . grateful.

Even a bit would still leave him ornery. But her day wasn't a total loss. She just learned he was going to be gone for a week. That sounded like heaven to her. Not that she had a heavy workload, but she didn't want him to question her about Charles. The only good thing was Charles worked for Lawson Steel. Max couldn't fire him like he had Sam. She'd still need to be cautious who saw them together, though.

She brought Max his coffee and put it on his desk. He never looked up at her as he took the cup and sipped. Rosslyn could tell from his face it wasn't her best. Max put the cup down and pushed it to the side.

"Worthless."

As she left the office she wasn't sure if he was talking about the coffee or her. In his eyes, they were probably the same. *An utter disappointment.*

Rosslyn didn't expect anything different, so it wasn't about to ruin her day. What was affecting her was Liz's absence. She was at least fun to talk to. Walking over to her desk she noticed Liz's personal things were still there. If a temp was arriving shortly, she didn't want them lying around. So she went over to the supply closet and found a half empty box. Removing the remaining contents, she headed back to Liz's desk. She collected the few family photos and trinkets she had hanging around. Inside the drawer were earrings, nail polish, and a few romance novels. By the time Rosslyn had compiled it all, the box was practically bursting at the seams.

Guess this is what you get when you're here for ten years. Ten long years.

Rosslyn would go crazy working for Max that long. A year seemed too much. But somehow she knew that wouldn't be a problem. Her time there was short-lived. Max or Laura would find something, and she'd be gone and cut off for good. Not that it was a bad thing, but she hoped to make enough money to cover the bills for a few months first. With not having to pay any rent right now, just about every penny was being utilized back home.

When she was home yesterday, she was thrilled to be able to hand her father eight hundred dollars. If she could do that every week, that would be perfect. The cost of living was so much cheaper back home. Since her father didn't have a mortgage or a car payment, all they needed were the basics. All this hassle wasn't for nothing.

She heard her phone ding, announcing a text. Rosslyn rushed over, hoping Max didn't hear it. The first thing she normally did was put her phone on silent. Before she could pick it up, another came through.

"You know the policy. No personal calls during business hours," Max snapped from his office.

There were rules on top of rules here. No one followed them. The game was not to get caught. She hit mute and then checked her messages anyway. *Thanks Liz. Are you trying to get me to join you on the unemployment line?*

CAN YOU PLEASE GET ALL MY THINGS BEFORE MR. ASSHOLE HAS THEM THROWN AWAY?

Rosslyn joyfully replied. ALREADY BOXED. I'LL TAKE IT HOME WITH ME TONIGHT.

YOU'RE THE BEST, ROSSLYN. WHY DIDN'T YOU START WORKING THERE TEN YEARS AGO?

Cause I'm not crazy. WASN'T MY TIME. GOT TO GO. I'LL CALL YOU TONIGHT.

Another ding. This time it was Charles.

HAVE A GOOD DAY.

She chuckled softly. It was so formal. He was back to being Charles, and Charlie was put away till the weekend. She was hoping to see him before that, but it had been left open last night. Probably because they were both so tired. Should she ask? No. Charles knew how to find her.

Replying she said, YOU TOO. It was simple and enough. The last thing she wanted to do was come off as some needy woman.

Actually a good morning text was more than she'd expected. She knew times had changed and people had casual sex. A one-night stand wasn't her style, and she hoped that wasn't what it had been. If it was, she'd accept it and move on. *But I'd miss him.*

It wasn't just the sex either. He made her laugh and somehow forget her troubles. Well, not forget, maybe they just didn't seem to weigh as much when he was around.

Screw it! Life was too damn short not to say what you want. Pulling out her phone again, she sent Charles another text.

WANT TO HAVE DINNER WITH ME THURSDAY NIGHT?

She would've said Friday but still hoped to return home for another visit yet a bit worried her father would believe that would become a weekly thing. It wasn't possible, and she surely wasn't going to ask Charles to take her each time. Although the perks definitely tempted her.

Charles replied. ONLY IF YOU HAVE DINNER WITH ME ON TUESDAY TOO.

She loved knowing he couldn't wait that long either.

Rosslyn giggled and then remembered where she was. Any sound of happiness would be a red flag that she was not concentrating on work. DEAL. GOT TO GO BEFORE I GET MY HEAD CHOPPED OFF.

She thought that would be the end of it. Instead of one last reply and a quick goodbye, he responded with PLEASE NOT THAT BEAUTIFUL HEAD OF YOURS. I'D MISS SEEING IT.

His words sent a warm feeling through her. *Beautiful.* Smiling, she slipped her phone inside her desk. This day just got a lot better, because she was seeing Charles again tomorrow. *Bring it on, Uncle Max. Whatever you say won't bother me today.*

She cursed herself, because shortly afterward he started barking orders faster than she could jot them down. The temp never showed up and somehow she seemed to be filling Liz's position. At this rate she actually was going to earn her paycheck. It felt good not to owe Uncle Max anything. Hopefully this was the way it would continue.

Charles tossed his phone on his desk and looked up at Gareth. "You couldn't wait till I called you?"

Gareth shook his head. "You're lucky I waited this long." He took a seat across from Charles and said, "I'm not even sure I believe what I found."

"Then maybe it's not true."

"It is. But it brings a hell of a lot of questions with it, and I'm not sure any of us are going to like the answers."

"I know you like to see if I can guess what you're talking about, but I'm not in the mood for games today." Actually he never was, but little sleep and Gareth interrupting his texting Rosslyn wasn't the way to start his day.

"We need to talk about our grandfather."

"You mentioned that already. He didn't like the Hendersons. That's not surprising. A lot of people don't. They can be difficult to work with."

"That's not what I'm talking about. The woman that was looking into our grandfather seemed to be doing some digging about Dad as well."

That was a new development. "What does Dad have to do with the Hendersons?"

"Nothing, I think. But I'm glad you're sitting down for this. Dad had an older sister. Her name was Audrey."

Sister? There never was any mention of that before. Actually, it was clear that their father was an only child. "Are you sure about that?"

"That woman, Gia Gravel, was the one who found the connection."

That wasn't an answer. Which meant Gareth wasn't willing to stake his name on it. "Is she a private investigator or something?" Charles asked.

Gareth shook his head. "Works for the Hendersons in the office. Before that she was a compliance auditor. I really can't tell you why she was looking into our family. My gut says it was at the request of the Hendersons."

In all those years, he couldn't even remember attending any functions that the Henderson family had been at also. They weren't on his radar as friends or enemies. "Why?"

"Why not? I figured at first she'd have to be connected to Maxwell somehow, but there was nothing."

"And nothing to the Hendersons either, right?"

Gareth shrugged. "She works for them."

In an office no different than Rosslyn. Not a threat. "And that is what makes you think Dad had a sister?" Charles saw nothing credible yet.

"You don't think it's odd that she looking into our family's past?"

Charles nodded. "We are a family in the public eye. People are always digging into our lives. You should know by now that half the shit they say isn't based on facts. If we back up a little and go with your theory that the Hendersons hired her to look into us, my question still would be why? Hendersons are not our rivals."

He could see Gareth was processing that question. "I never thought of that. I'll need to check," Gareth said.

"You're losing me, Gareth," Charles said, grumbling his frustration with the entire conversation.

"You're right about the Hendersons, but what if they're connected to Grayson? Maxwell could've asked the Henderson family to dig into ours."

Charles burst out laughing. "Gareth, you need to take a break. I know I'm the one who asked you to get me all the dirt you can on Maxwell, but I think you're seeing things that aren't there."

"So you don't believe Dad had a sister?" Gareth leaned over to rest his forearms on his knees.

Charles wasn't sure what to believe. A secret like this being hidden all these years wouldn't have been easy. That doesn't mean it was done. "I don't know. Back then the mortality rate wasn't like it is today. Since Dad never mentioned her, he might not remember. I don't see the point of dredging up the past. Not unless there is a damn good reason we need to."

"I can't believe what I'm hearing. If anyone in this family should want to know, I'd think it was you."

"Why? Because I'm the oldest?" Charles asked.

"Because you're the one closest to Dad."

That was still a misconception even now. No one was

close to their father. He was always there and they never questioned his love, but no one really knew him at all. Their father was a closed book. *And if there was a sister, that should remain closed as well.*

"Then trust me when I say Dad wouldn't want us prying into the past. Besides, we have a future we're supposed to be working on. We don't have time for a wild-goose chase."

"Damn it. I really thought that woman Gia might be on to something. But you're right. We're the future of Lawson Steel. The only thing that matters are the decisions the six of us make. Right now, I'm deciding I'm going for a late breakfast. Want to join me?"

"I have a lot of work to do," Charles answered.

Gareth laughed. "You always do. But somehow this weekend you didn't. I wonder why? If you came to breakfast with me we could discuss it."

From outside of the office, Seth popped his head in. "What are we discussing over breakfast?"

"Charles's girlfriend," Gareth shouted.

Charles glared at him and said, "We're not in high school. She's not my *girlfriend.*"

Gareth shrugged. "Lady friend. Is that better?"

Seth entered the office and said, "When the hell did you find time to meet someone? Every time I talk to you, you're busy working." Then Seth slapped Gareth on the back. "Oh, I get it. He's *working.* All this time I felt as though I wasn't pulling my weight around here."

"Let's get something straight. *You're not.* And I *was* working. I had a date this weekend. That's all. Now if you two don't mind, I do have things I need to take care of this morning."

Seth turned to Gareth and asked, "How come you know about her?"

Gareth answered, "Nothing slips by me."

"That's because your inflated ego blocks it," Seth teased.

Charles fought to hold back his laughter. Seth was always able to knock Gareth down a peg or two. Thankfully, because Gareth at times was overconfident.

"Is there a family meeting no one invited me to?" Dylan asked from the door.

Really? Doesn't anyone fucking work around here? "They were just leaving."

"Yeah. We're going to breakfast to discuss Charles's romantic weekend," Seth said.

This was getting out of control. If he didn't put an end to it, they'd have him married off by lunch. He stood up and pointed at the door. "See it? Close it on your way out."

Dylan looked at both Seth and Gareth and said, "Pissing him off so early is usually my job. What did you guys do?"

"It wasn't me," Gareth said.

"Enough!" Charles barked. "My relationship is none of your business. If you have any questions or comments, keep them to your fucking self. This is not social hour. We're running a business. Seth, you were supposed to have a file on my desk first thing this morning. Do you have it?"

Seth held it up. "That's why I'm here."

"Good. Dylan, any luck with negotiating pricing the electrical for the Smith's job next week?"

Dylan nodded. "Another six thousand dollars taken off the labor side while still using top quality products."

"Great," Charles said. Then he looked at Gareth. "Guess you're free to go have breakfast now."

Gareth got up, shaking his head. "Damn, I hope I never get as old and ornery as you, Charles."

Seth said in a softer voice, "Maybe he's missing his girl."

The three of them left his office laughing. Charles wasn't.

He didn't know where things were going with Rosslyn yet, and his brothers didn't know when to shut up. He would need to make sure they didn't bump into any of them when they were out. If they did, the ribbing was going to get a lot worse.

Hell, who am I kidding? Gareth is going to run his fucking mouth at breakfast and probably show them her picture. He just hoped Gareth didn't tell them where she worked. It would go from laughter to lecture quickly. Charles didn't want to hear it. He already knew he was playing with fire. But there was another fire he couldn't ignore. And even now, he missed her.

I should've asked her to dinner tonight instead.

Charles walked over and closed his office door. Even though he told Gareth not to worry about whatever Gia Gravel had uncovered, he had some concerns. If his father had a sister, what happened to her? Why didn't the family ever speak of her?

He was about to do something he told Gareth not to. He looked up the number and then called Henderson Corporation. When the operator answered he said, "Gia Gravel please."

"One moment."

When he was transferred, she answered. "Hello, this is Gia."

"Hello. My name is Charles Lawson. Do you have a moment to talk?"

"Lawson? I'm sorry, but do I know you?"

"I'm not sure. That's why I'm calling," Charles said.

"Sorry sir, I'm a bit confused. Are you a client of the Hendersons?" Gia asked.

"No. I was given your name, and they thought you were trying to get in touch with me. Or maybe my grandfather."

There was a long pause, and then she said, "I wasn't

looking for anyone in particular. Just looking at old photos. I do that a lot. It's possible I may have come across one with your name, or maybe your grandfather's. I like old things."

This was sounding more like a coincidence than anything else. That's not saying she didn't unknowingly uncover something about his family that should be left buried. The question was, who might she have told? Hopefully no one.

Playing it off, Charles said, "I'm not that old, so you must have been looking for another Charles Lawson. Sorry for taking up your time."

"Not a problem at all. Have a wonderful day, Mr. Lawson."

"You too," Charles said and ended the call.

Until he met Rosslyn, Charles never believed in coincidence or fate. No such thing as luck either. A person made his path in life by the choices he made. But Rosslyn wasn't part of his plan. If anything, she was going against it. So what brought them together? One accidental meeting and then another, until finally he needed to speak to her. If that wasn't fate, what was?

He didn't believe Gia was searching for any malicious reason. She just happened to stumble across something no one else had. Charles didn't need to know any more than that. This was done as far as he was concerned. Hopefully it was for Gareth as well.

Charles opened his laptop to finally start working when his cell phone rang. "Sal, let me guess, your mother called."

"Over and over again. Thanks for riling her up. She's even talking to me about grandkids again."

Charles laughed. "Wow. It's worse than I thought."

"I thought we had a deal. We never take our dates there."

"It slipped my mind," Charles said. He knew it was the

one place he could take Rosslyn where she'd feel relaxed. It turned out he was right.

"That's why I'm calling. She must be something else for you to forget things like that. Where did you meet her?"

"Would you believe me if I told you on the street?"

Sal laughed. "That doesn't sound good. Unless she's a—"

"No! She's not. Actually she works for Maxwell Grayson."

"Hell no. And you're dating her? You know her job will be gone when he finds out. Please tell me you're not dating her just to fuck with him. I'm sure it's tempting, but that'd be fucking wrong. And my mother would have your hide too."

"I'm not that big of an asshole. I actually like her. She's different." It was the first time he'd admitted that she meant something to him.

"Since you took her to my parents' restaurant, I knew that. Just wasn't sure you did," Sal said.

"The timing sucks. Remember I told you I was going to make him regret what he did to my father?"

"You mean you're actually going after Grayson?" Sal asked.

"I am."

"Since I am still a police officer, you might not want to tell me too much," Sal warned.

Charles laughed. "I'm not breaking the law. This isn't going to be some street fight. Everything I have will be turned over to the Feds."

"Damn it, Charles, you better be prepared for the repercussions. I'm not the law in the city and can't help you if he retaliates."

"Someone has to stop him."

"Just watch your back, Charles. Grayson doesn't play by the rules. That gives him the edge. Make sure you have everything lined up before going to the Feds. Hell, I'm not sure he doesn't have a few of them in his pocket."

That was a fear Charles had as well. "Do you want to look at the files I have?"

There was a pause and then Sal said, "I'd do anything for you, Charles, you know that. In this instance, I'm thinking it would be best if I kept my distance."

"Worried about what you'll see?"

"No. But if I'm brought into a court of law, I don't want them to be able to use me against you."

Sal was right. And Maxwell might dig enough to find the connection between Sal and him. How would Sal explain he knew of the illegal activity and did nothing? *I can't have Sal become another one of Maxwell's victims.*

"Then let's talk about something else. And not Rosslyn either."

"Since I'm on duty, you're lucky, because I can't talk long. We'll catch up soon. But do me a favor. Take your sweetie someplace else for a while. Maybe my mother will start complaining about you instead of me."

"You got it," Charles said and ended the call. Where was he going to take Rosslyn for dinner tomorrow then?

Leaning back in his chair, he smiled. *Take out.* He didn't normally take women to his place. Definitely not for an overnighter. There was no indication that she'd be opposed to staying, but then again, he hadn't asked either. *Maybe I shouldn't assume, and let it take its natural course.*

But he missed having her in his arms. Kissing her good-night in front of her building was not how he'd wanted last night to end. He didn't want a repeat tomorrow either.

Oh Rosslyn, what are you doing to me? Sal was right. This girl was special, and he wanted to make sure she knew it.

How was it she was working harder with Max gone than when he was there? Of course that meant her day flew by. But it also meant she needed to work late to get things completed.

Charles had texted her earlier saying he'd pick her up at six. But it was already after five and she hadn't left yet. The option was she meet him someplace or cancel. Neither was how she planned the night to go.

Rosslyn didn't want to send a text. So she decided to call him instead.

"Hi. Is everything okay?" Charles asked.

With a heavy sigh she said, "No. I'm still at work. I might not get out till six. By the time I go home and take care of the cat, it'll be late. Maybe we should—"

"We can have dinner at my house."

"Charles, that won't change anything. It will be so late and—"

"You can stay the night. I'll take you by to take care of the cat in the morning before you go to work."

Rosslyn was so tempted to say yes. There was nothing more she wanted than to spend a night in his arms. But working the next day with hardly any sleep wasn't the best way to show Uncle Max she was qualified to do the job.

"How about a compromise?" she asked.

"What it is?"

"Have me home by midnight?" That sounded reasonable, just not as much fun.

"I can do that."

"Great. So how about picking me up at seven instead?"

Charles grumbled. "Now you're pushing it. But okay. How do you feel about Thai food?"

"Never had it," she said. "But willing to give it a try. Just nothing too spicy."

"Okay. I'll pick it up on my way to grab you."

"I'll be ready." She ended the call so she could finish the last few things on her list. But it wasn't easy with her mind still on Charles. She knew he was trying to give them as much time together as he could. That was sweet. It showed he was missing her too.

She was finally done and closing her laptop when the phone rang. She was so tempted not to answer, but who could be calling the office at this hour?

"Mr. Grayson's office, this is Rosslyn, may I help you?"

"I just sent you an email. Make sure you have everything taken care of first thing in the morning."

"Of course. Anything else?"

"There's a lot riding on this. Don't be late." Max ended the call before she could reply.

Gee, you're welcome. No. I don't mind working late. I know how much you appreciate me going the extra mile. Errr. That man was so damn rude. How did Liz do it for so long? Rosslyn didn't care how good the money was, if she took this too long, she might start to lose her self-respect. She had to get out of here before that happened.

She couldn't do it tonight, but tomorrow she needed to look at her finances and her options. No matter what Max was going to do, she knew she needed to look for another job. One where she was free to date Charles. It shouldn't be her employer's choice or anyone else's. This was between two grown adults who really . . . *enjoy being together.*

Grabbing her purse, she headed to the elevator before the phone rang again. Although she felt bad about not spending serious quality time with Miss Snuggles, Rosslyn knew she was going to only have time to feed her, give her a quick pet, and get in the shower. She might be wrong, but she didn't think Charles was going to have them eat Thai food in his car. If he was taking her back to his place, there might be dessert on the menu too.

She rushed so much that she got a cramp in her right calf. It was horrible and she needed to kick off her shoes and try to walk it out. Charles must've pulled up just in time to see the sight.

"Are you okay?" he asked, practically picking her up into his arms.

"Yes. Just a cramp."

"Cramp?" Charles asked.

She tried joking, hoping it would ease the pain a bit. "Yes, a Charlie horse."

Charles didn't laugh. Instead he asked, "Where and I'll rub it."

"Don't you dare touch it! It hurts," she exclaimed.

He placed her in the passenger seat and then ran around the car to the driver's side. "I know what you need."

"It'll be fine. It's just a cramp." She hoped he wasn't rushing her off to the hospital or something.

"I have a Jacuzzi. The hot water and jets will ease the pain. It'll only take a few minutes to get there."

Knowing they were on the way to his place wasn't helping ease her tension, but it was a damn good way to distract her from the pain. When she moved her leg, it tensed up again and she winced.

"Almost there," Charles said.

"Charles, slow down. This is not a medical emergency. I'm okay," she stressed once again.

"Rosslyn, you're in pain."

She reached out and placed her hand on his thigh. "Not as much as I'm going to be if we get in an accident."

Charles did as she asked, but his focus didn't change. Within minutes they were parked in front of one of the tallest buildings in the city. "Where are we?"

"My apartment. Or at least we will be once I get you inside." Charles called over a man standing in the doorway. "I need you to park it. Then bring up the bags in the back."

"Yes sir." The man took the keys.

Charles came around to the passenger side and said, "Hold on. Let me carry you."

Rosslyn put her hands up. "I am not letting you carry me anywhere."

"It'll hurt less," Charles said.

"Not my pride. Haven't you ever had a cramp? I need to walk it off. It'll be fine. I forgot to change my shoes and did all the rushing around on heels. Now I'm paying for it. It's life's way of reminding you not to do that again."

The man waited, holding the keys as though he wasn't sure what to do. Once Rosslyn was out of the car, he got inside and drove away.

"Oh, my purse. It's in your car."

"He'll bring it up too," Charles said.

"I guess if you can trust him with your car, I won't panic

about the few bucks in my wallet," she teased as they went through the lobby.

"He's paid to keep this place secure. Stealing any amount would be foolish."

She shook her head. "I was joking."

"Sorry. I take the safety of this place and the people in it, very seriously."

I guess so. As she made it to the elevator and the doors closed, she finally took a moment to gain her bearings. There was a sign on the front of the building. What did it say? As she thought back, it came to her. *Lawson Steel.*

"Charles, what are we doing here?"

"I live here," he replied.

"At work? Why?"

He shrugged. "It's convenient."

"Maybe for your boss. No wonder you're stuck working all the time. You have no place to hide." But as the elevator continued going up, she realized he didn't just have an apartment in the building; it was the penthouse. She shot him a look and the word slipped from her lips. "Lawson." It wasn't a question. Just a realization. One she wasn't sure how to deal with.

He looked at her and asked, "You didn't know?"

She shook her head. "No." Rosslyn wasn't sure why his last name never came up before now. Was that an intentional act on his part of just an oversight? She shouldn't be pointing fingers at Charles. She never even asked.

Charles looked down at her. "Does it matter?"

Rosslyn honestly didn't know. But now it made sense why Uncle Max told her never to speak to him. Charles was her uncle's competition. There was an awful feeling in the pit of her stomach. Had he sought her out because she worked for his competition? Was any of this real? Could he be using her to get to her uncle?

There were too many questions she didn't have answers to. But asking them while in his apartment wasn't going to work for her either. She needed to think. Sort things out.

"Charles, I think I should go home."

He reached out for her. "Rosslyn, this doesn't change anything. It's just a name."

She looked up at him and wanted to believe that. But Lawson wasn't just any name. It was tied to wealth she couldn't relate to. He had money like her uncle. And she was definitely out of his class. They were enjoying each other now. But this wouldn't last. Eventually he'd grow tired of playing with a small town girl.

"No Charles. Clark is just a name. Lawson is an empire."

"Rosslyn, this changes nothing." Charles reached up and touched her cheek. "I'm still Charles."

But you're not Charlie. "I want to believe that."

"Then stay. Have dinner with me. And let's talk."

She wanted to run all the way back home to Alexandria Bay. But even there she wouldn't be able to hide from how she felt. That would remind her of how sweet it could've been between them. Why did hearing his last name seem to spoil it all?

All she could think of was how he must have laughed at her when she packed their pathetic picnic lunch. He probably travels all over the world doing all kinds of wild and exciting things and I take him to sit and watch kites. If she'd known then . . . *I never would've said yes to lunch and never had one of the best weeks of my life.*

She could walk away, but she'd still have her memories. That probably was the worst part. She now knew what she'd miss. Rosslyn knew what being a Lawson meant to the world, but she just wanted the guy who made her laugh, brightened her days.

Rosslyn knew this was an impossible situation, but she'd stay and talk. Then she was going back to the apartment. *An apartment that isn't even mine. God, we are from two different worlds.* She looked into his eyes and hated for this dream to come to an end.

"Okay, I'll stay. But I make no promises," Rosslyn said.

Charles leaned over and said, "I do. I promise, Rosslyn, I'm not out to hurt you." He kissed her gently and added, "And you know deep in your heart, I'm not lying."

I know I want that to be true. More than I've ever wanted anything. Thankfully before she could answer, there was a knock on the door. Charles released her as he went to answer. When he returned he said, "We can continue this conversation as we eat."

Somehow no matter what she ate, it wasn't going to agree with her. Her stomach was doing more flips than a gymnast. *Who knows? Maybe there's a fortune cookie in there that will have some good advice for me.* Because right now she had no idea what the hell to do. Follow her heart or follow her head? It was an internal battle that she didn't think was going to end, no matter what Charles said to her tonight.

The look on her face when she realized who he was, was going to haunt him for days. Charles thought for sure she was going to get right back on that elevator and leave. He couldn't blame her. It wasn't as though he'd lied, but at no point had he prepared her for it either.

Now here they were, sitting in his kitchen, and he had no idea where to start. Charles couldn't tell her what his initial thoughts about her had been. Even now, he was pissed at himself for even thinking she was a . . . *Don't fucking even think it again.*

They sat eating in silence. This wasn't going to play out well. It would drive a wedge between them if he didn't somehow fix it. "I'm sorry."

She looked up at him and said, "For being a Lawson?"

That was the one thing he couldn't change. Actually he didn't want to either. He was proud of all his ancestors had built. As he looked at the skyline of the city, it was like looking at their legacy. The Lawsons had been building in New York since the 1800s and they were only getting bigger, stronger. For all he knew, she didn't know any of that either. And from the look on her face, the steel business was the last thing on her mind.

"I'm proud of my name as you are of yours. It's part of who we are. Just not everything we are."

"You're right. But it explains why Mr. Grayson didn't want me speaking to you. He . . . sorry to say this, but he hates your guts."

Charles chuckled. "That is something I already knew. There is a history between the families. And that's not all." *Hell, none of it was.* She didn't need to know the details. Unfortunately, once the Feds had the file, the world was going to get an up-close look at Maxwell. They were all in for a shock.

"So you see why we shouldn't be sitting here right now."

"It hasn't stopped us before. What is different?" Charles asked.

She looked around the room and then turned back to him. "This. All of this."

"My kitchen is the deal breaker?" he asked jokingly. That was a stupid thing to say, because she wasn't in the mood for laughter.

Her tone took a higher pitch as she said, "This has nothing to do with appliances, Charles, and you know it. I'm a girl from a small town who likes living in her small world. You create big cities. You're always striving for bigger, grander, higher. We're nothing at all alike."

Charles needed to keep the focus away from Lawson Steel and on him. "I'm the guy who enjoys the fireworks in a park. Who likes PB&J. And looks forward to hearing your voice and seeing your face. If you question that, think back to the stories Mama told you. I'm *that* guy." He hated saying it, but had to. "I'm Charlie."

Rosslyn sat staring at him. "You look like him, act like him, and talk like him. But I don't know which is real and which isn't. No one can live two lives for long. One always consumes the other. And to be honest, Charles, I can't see Charlie being the winner of that battle."

Damn her. It was a reality he didn't want to face either. Since taking over as CEO, the fun, easy-going Charlie seemed to have almost vanished. It wasn't until he met Rosslyn that he'd desired slowing down a bit and enjoying life. He'd been pushing full speed ahead with one goal: bring Lawson Steel to number one, worldwide. Fun? There was no time for that shit. Yet, somehow she had him squeezing some in. It felt damn good.

Rosslyn worked for Maxwell, so she knew what it took to manage companies like these. Although their tactics were very different, their drive and dedication to succeed wasn't.

She was sexy and beautiful and so damn insightful as well. She wasn't a prize to be won. Sal's mother had been right, Rosslyn was a gem to be treasured. He'd been trying to avoid talking about certain things so as to not fuck things up between them. The lack of being forthcoming, might be his downfall. Charles tried calculating risk as he would in a business deal. A relationship, not that he was ready to define this as such, was a hell of a lot more complex. *Makes my contracts easy to figure out.*

All he needed was to think of some way to prove to her he was a blend of both. If not, he might just lose her. *Hell, who am I kidding? Rosslyn is too damn good for me. But I'll be damned if I'm just going to let her walk out of my life. Not without a fight.*

There was no flower or gift that would show her how special she was to him. She wasn't materialistic. But he wasn't Mr. Romantic, so the words didn't flow from him like a poem either. Hell, he couldn't even find the right words to explain what was going on within him right now.

Panic? Desperation? Fear? Over losing a woman I met about a week ago? Am I nuts? Have I totally lost my mind?

This line of thinking didn't fit his character at all. Then again, neither did taking off for a weekend to meet someone's parents. It was like she had spiked his drink, and it had a long-lasting effect. Charles wasn't sure how or when that happened. It felt like he was on a construction site and someone whacked him in the back of the head with a two-by-four board. The wind was knocked out of him, his head spinning, making him feel a bit dazed. A very unfamiliar feeling.

Talking her into staying for dinner gave him some hope. Yet the look in her eyes said she really didn't want to be there. He could only imagine what Rosslyn was feeling right now. *God, she probably doesn't trust a thing I say.*

"I'm not going to lie to you, Rosslyn. I should've told you before, but things were so comfortable between us that I didn't want that to change."

"They were," Rosslyn said softly. "But now I realize there is so much I don't know about you. It's like we jumped from A to Z."

"And you regret it?" He hoped to hell she didn't. Charles had a few regrets but not over what they had shared together. It had been amazing.

"No. If I had to do it over, I would. But I just wish that . . . that we were more compatible."

"I thought we were. What changed? The fact that I'm the CEO of Lawson Steel?"

"CEO? You mean—Oh God, that's even worse than I thought," she said, her eyes wide in shock. "I thought maybe you worked for your father or something."

"I did. He retired a few years ago and my five brothers and I run it. Being the oldest, and most experienced, I fell into the CEO role." There was a lot more to it, but for now, it explained some of the dynamics.

"So you're not just his rival, but you're his . . . equal."

She was once again comparing him to Maxwell. He didn't like his name in the same sentence as the scumbag. Usually his focus was on Maxwell too, but right now, Charles wanted him out of this conversation. He reached across the table and touched her hand. "Let's start again. I'm Charles J Lawson the Seventh. I'm thirty-eight years old. I'm a Leo. My favorite food is whatever someone else cooks for me. I like to do just about anything outdoors except jog or run, never saw the point. When I was younger and had more time, I played the saxophone and dreamed of being in a band. I'm not because it sounded better in my head than my music teacher told me it actually was. So I did what came natural and followed in my family's footsteps. Now I run Lawson Steel. And what about you?"

He saw her lips slightly curl a few times, which was a positive sign. *And she didn't pull away from my touch.*

"Fine. Okay. I'm Rosslyn Clark, and I'm thirty-one, but I only admit to being twenty-nine. I'm an only child, which you know. I grew up in Alexandria Bay, which you know. My parents, you have met." She glared at him and continued, "Somehow you knew a lot more about me than I did you."

"I'm trying to correct that." So far it seemed to be working. A two-way conversation was a hell of a lot better than the alternative. The dreaded silence treatment.

"You are. I'm glad. Let's see. You know I don't like living in the city and that my tastes are . . . simple. What you don't know is I can cook a lot more than a PB&J, given enough time."

Charles smiled. "I don't know, strawberry jam is my favorite."

"Maybe your taste is a lot simpler than I thought," Rosslyn said.

"Can you do me a favor?" Charles asked.

She shrugged. "Maybe with a bit more details, I can answer that."

"Date me for a week. Don't think about my name or my title. Let's just be us."

"You're serious, aren't you?" Rosslyn asked.

He stroked her hand with his thumb. "Go to dinner with me tomorrow."

"Charles, we're having dinner now. Or at least we're supposed to be," Rosslyn said.

Their food was cold on the plate and he didn't care. "This didn't turn out the way I thought it would."

"And how was that?" Rosslyn asked.

With you in my arms all night. "Relaxing, like the rest of our dates." A much better choice of words, he thought. The last thing he needed was for her to think this was all about sex. Amazing as it was, there was more to this than just that.

"What do you suggest?"

This is where it got tricky. The wrong choice could end

up in a refusal. He needed to keep it simple, yet not so much that it looked like he was trying too hard. "I've been dying for pizza. I mean the deep dish loaded to the max with extra cheese." He could almost see her mouth watering. *Nailed it.*

"Okay. But I have one confession."

At this point, unless she told him she was married, nothing else mattered. "What is it?"

"I like thin crust."

He pretended to be wounded and said, "Oh, the pain." Then he laughed. "I don't see an issue with that, since I can eat a pizza all by myself."

"Not if Mama was cooking it," Rosslyn said.

"That's because restaurants normally just refill your beverage. She believes no one should see the bottom of the plate."

"Okay. Even though I love it there, maybe we can find a place in the city."

"There's a few I frequent. It is another one of my weaknesses."

"You weren't kidding. You like anything you don't have to cook," she teased.

There was a sense of relief that he'd been able to not only secure another date, but see that beautiful smile of hers again. Not a forced, trying-to-be-polite one either. He might not have known her long, but there were certain things she couldn't hide.

The only major issue he could foresee now was her reaction when the Feds eventually showed up at Grayson Corp. Absolutely, without a doubt, this was not the time to inform her of Maxwell's doings. And on top of that, his part in Maxwell's downfall would tip the scale in the wrong direction for sure.

"I don't know about you, but if I'm going to eat cold

food, it's going to be ice cream. How do you feel about tossing this and taking a ride for a sundae?"

"Whip cream and nuts?" Rosslyn inquired.

Nodding he said, "Hot fudge and a cherry too."

For the first time since Rosslyn learned who he was, her fingers were playfully entangled with his. It wasn't even close to what he wanted, but it was going to have to do. *Damn it.* He never knew that not holding someone could actually physically hurt. Hopefully they would be past all this soon.

He never thought he'd find someone like her, now he had to figure out how to hold on to her.

"I know, Dad. I'm going to try to come back home this weekend. Uncle Max is traveling with Aunt Laura and isn't due back until early next week."

"Must be nice not to have a care in the world," he said.

"Dad, that's the problem, they don't care. Not about anything." Not about their employees, and definitely not about his sister. She thought for sure Aunt Laura would've asked how they were, or at least said to tell them hello. But not one word, as though they didn't exist. That was so difficult for Rosslyn to comprehend. There wasn't a birthday or holiday that went by without her mother sending Uncle Max and Aunt Laura a card. *Cards that probably went in the trash. Wouldn't shock me if they weren't even opened.*

"You might not understand it or like it, sweet pea, but their relationship works for them."

"I'm not sure that's what I'd call it, Dad. You should hear how they talk to each other. I wish I could tell them if they don't have something nice to say then zip it." She couldn't believe people who were supposed to have such class, didn't seem to have any when it came to each other.

"I know it's not easy, but they are your family. Your mother would want you to treat them with respect."

Even though she gets none. I know Dad. Mom is my hero too. She was blessed being raised by people with such high morals. Through their struggles came strength and perseverance. Rosslyn hoped some of that had rubbed off onto her. From what she was going through, she was going to need it.

But her dad was right. This wasn't about them; it was about her. She'd heard worse from strangers and ignored it. She just needed to do the same with them. *They're practically strangers anyway. I know their names. Wow. That's really personal.*

"I won't let Mom down. How is she doing, by the way?"

"She's here and would like to talk to you. Do you have time?"

She didn't care if the President or Pope was standing there, needing something. This was the moment she yearned for. Her mother knew who she was. "I've got all the time she needs."

When her mother came on the phone, Rosslyn had to choke back the tears. "How is my little Rosie?"

It was the pet name only her mother called her. It seemed like ages since she'd heard it. "I'm great, Mom." She knew better than to ask how she was doing. Actually she learned not to ask her mother any questions as it sometimes confused her. So she told her things instead. "I went out last night and I had the best homemade ice cream ever."

"Hot fudge or caramel?"

Rosslyn giggled. "Both. It was amazing. Of course I am not sure my pants fit the same today."

"Rosie, you know you've always had a sweet tooth and never gained a pound. You're just like your father. But your father seems to be eating better now. I saw him eat wheat toast."

"Watch out, Mom. Next will be prunes for breakfast." She knew her father was listening so he could decipher what was true or not from the call later.

As usual her mother switched subjects. "I met the nicest man yesterday. I think he would be perfect for you."

I thought I had met one myself. Now I'm not so sure.

Since her mother didn't go out except to the doctors, she had no idea who she was talking about. "That's nice."

"I told your father we should have him over for dinner. What time do you think you'll be home tonight?"

And there it goes. The moment was already slipping away. "Not sure. I might have to work late. You and Dad eat and we can do it another time."

"Okay Rosie, that sounds good."

"Mom, I have to go back to work now." She knew it was time to say goodbye. Never an easy thing.

"What time will you be home for dinner tonight?" her mother asked again.

"Very late, Mom. I love you, but I have to go." *Before I start crying.*

"I love you too, my little Rosie."

Before the phone call ended her father came back on the line. "It's okay, sweet pea. Your mother is going to go watch her game shows now. You get back to work and we'll talk tomorrow."

"Dad, are you sure you don't want me to come home?" He always told her no, but she knew how hard this was on him as well. At least with her there, he could go out for a while. Maybe work on a boat or two. Just for his sanity alone.

"In sickness and in health, sweet pea." Then he ended the call.

Will someone ever love me the way you love Mom? God, I hope so. She also hoped if she did find someone, their love would never be tested as her parents' had been.

There was a brief moment when she and Charles were together in Alexandria Bay, that she'd let herself daydream what it would be like if they were together. Not married, but an actual couple. They could go out on the sailboat and watch the stars at night. But Alexandria Bay must have bored him. It's beautiful and great for boating and fishing, but when you're used to the lights and sounds of the city, one would grow tired of hearing crickets and frogs at night.

She had called her father because she needed his advice. If he knew who Charles was would he have still welcomed him into the house? *What am I talking about? Of course he would. Dad's awesome. He doesn't have a mean bone in his body, just like Mom.*

Rosslyn needed to think along the same lines as her parents. Charles wasn't rich and powerful. He was just a man who knew how to make her laugh and smile. That's all he should be judged on, right? It definitely shouldn't have anything to do with how Uncle Max felt. If so, Charles would be considered the devil himself.

So without being able to talk to her father and with no sisters to call, she had to think of someone who'd listen. Brandy wasn't going to be impartial. She may have heard the bed rocking a bit more than it should've on their stay in Alexandria Bay. Brandy would say anyone who can make someone scream like that was a keeper.

Taking money, prestige, and sex off the list left the things she already knew and liked about him. There really wasn't any reason to overthink it. They were going out for pizza tonight, and she just wanted to enjoy it. What else could happen?

She looked up at the ceiling and said, "Please universe, let this be it. I really need a break."

Charles had asked for one week. That's something she could commit to. Her one fear was becoming even more emotionally invested and then having to face that it wasn't going to work out. He wasn't the first guy she'd been involved with, but he had the potential of being the one who would break her heart.

She wasn't sure which scared her more, that he could be the love of her life, or they find out that no matter how good it was between them, they weren't compatible? At least all the cards were on the table and in one week, they would . . .? *Who the heck knows what tonight will bring, never mind a week.*

If she didn't stop worrying about next week, how was she ever going to be able to enjoy tonight?

Rosslyn looked at the clock again and it seemed to have stopped. There's no way it was only noon. Yesterday she was so busy the entire day flew by. Today, nothing. If she thought there weren't cameras hidden somewhere spying on the staff, she'd pull out her phone and read a book, play a game, or just catch up on what's happening on social media. She was so out of the loop, but as long as she was in the building, that wasn't going to change.

She'd had four cups of coffee already and they were no longer helping. There really was no need for her to sit at a desk when no one called. All calls except Uncle Max's were being diverted to the operator who redirected them to God knows who. Rosslyn was on a need to know basis and obviously she didn't need to know a damn thing. *All I have to do is show up.*

There was no better time to grab lunch than the present. But as soon as she pulled her purse from the desk drawer, the phone rang. She knew exactly who it was, but still answered the same. "Mr. Grayson's office, this is Rosslyn, how may I help you?"

"I'm expecting a delivery today. I want you to call me immediately upon delivery. I'll give you further instructions then," Max barked.

"Yes, sir."

He hung up and she placed her purse back in the drawer. It would just be her luck that it came as soon as she left the office. There was no way she was getting her butt chewed out for leaving her post unattended. That didn't mean she wasn't going to play a bit on the computer.

She needed to start looking for an apartment. It was something she'd procrastinated about for too long. Maybe because her gut said she wasn't going to require one. She had never been fired from a job before, but then again, Max wanted perfection. That didn't exist. Just in case she didn't screw up and still had a job in two weeks, she was going to need a place to lay her head. It didn't need to be much. Actually it couldn't be, or she wouldn't have any money to send home. So she started looking at one bedroom places. She practically passed out when she saw the rental fees. She didn't need anything that big so she refined her search to efficiency apartments. They were out of her price range as well. So she went into the one thing she didn't want to do, rent a room in someone else's place.

Not that she was afraid to share a place, but living with someone she didn't know bothered her. What if they had disgusting habits she couldn't ignore? She'd be stuck in a lease with no way out. And the ones she found on the internet weren't in neighborhoods like where Mama had her restaurant. If there was a loud boom, it wasn't going to be from a fireworks celebration.

She was done looking. So far, running by the seat of her pants had worked out. Something would come up. Maybe there would be another apartment that needed to be watched. *Wonder if Miss Snuggles would give me a letter of recommendation?*

Rosslyn laughed, thinking how pissed off the cat looked this morning before she left for work. She knew cats didn't like water, but she figured they were smart enough not to walk into a shower that was turned on. That fluff ball Persian looked a lot smaller dripping wet. After a quick towel dry, she looked a bit better, but would need to be combed out tonight.

Rosslyn knew exactly what Miss Snuggles felt like. Her hair wasn't naturally straight. More like naturally frizzy. It had been really humid when she walked to work this morning and she felt like a hot mess. It was an exaggeration, but she knew she was going to shower again before her date tonight. *Guess I'll be doing more than just the cat's hair before I go out.*

Thankfully one of the security guards came up to the office and said, "I was told to deliver this to Mr. Grayson's office personally."

"Thank you. I'll inform him that it has arrived."

She took the large envelop and went back to her desk. Max answered on the first ring. "You have it?"

"I do," she replied.

"Go into my office and put it in the top right drawer. Then be sure to lock my office when you exit."

"Okay. Is there anything else you need me to do?"

"Go home."

"Now?" There were still three hours left before her workday ended.

"You're not going to be needed for anything else today.

141

Don't worry, you'll still receive a *full* day's pay." She didn't miss the snide tone.

Oh how she wished she could tell him she didn't need his money. However, the fact was, she did. "Thank you. Please call me if anything changes and I'll return."

"Trust me, you're not needed."

And trust me, I feel it. Hanging up the phone, she let out a heavy sigh. She'd worked late yesterday without additional pay, so he really wasn't granting her anything she hadn't earned. But Max had to make sure he belittled her any way he could, from her looks to her intelligence. Eventually, he was going to run out of things to complain about.

What will we talk about then? Maybe he'll have to start complimenting me instead. Hell was going to freeze over before something nice came out of that man's mouth.

She went into his office and put the large envelope in the drawer as directed. Once she triple checked his office was locked, she grabbed her purse and headed to the elevator. She had no idea what came over her, but she could only imagine Uncle Max's face if he knew she wasn't going home to twiddle her thumbs. She had a date with one hot and sexy Charles Lawson, and Uncle Max was paying her to get ready for it. *Thanks, Uncle Max.*

Charles was surprised Rosslyn had texted him saying she was out of work early. That wasn't like Maxwell. What the hell was the guy up to? The tabloids posted a photo seemingly showing Maxwell and Laura off celebrating their fortieth wedding anniversary. That was definitely set up as a distraction, and it was making him nervous.

On the way to pick up Rosslyn, he called Gareth. "Got a job for you."

"Rosslyn has a girlfriend and you want to set me up on a blind date?" Gareth joked.

"You'll be lucky to meet her, never mind any of her friends. But no, this has to do with Maxwell."

"Not as much fun, but interesting. What do you need?"

"I want to know what he's really up to."

"Don't buy all that lovey dovey shit on the news today?"

"Not for a second. Oddly, he sent Rosslyn home early, with pay."

"Damn. That's more surprising than the photos with Laura. What do you think he's up to?" Gareth asked.

Charles growled. "That's what I just asked you to find out."

Gareth laughed. "And what will you be doing while I'm *working?*"

Wishing I had only four brothers instead of five. It was evident that Gareth could never work for Charles because if he wasn't challenging everything Charles said, he was joking around about what Charles was doing. There was no winning with him.

Charles didn't bother pretending. "I'll be having dinner with Rosslyn. So don't call unless it's important."

"Where are you going?"

"Why?" Charles asked.

"In case I get hungry doing my research. Can't a guy snag a free dinner?"

"Of course you can. Just not with us," Charles said. "I'm sure Seth would enjoy chatting with you again. You two seem to enjoy discussing my love life."

"Love? Did the great Charles Lawson just use the word love?"

"Gareth, it was a figure of speech. Or in this instance a back-the-fuck-up-and-stay-out-of-my-personal-life warning."

Gareth laughed. "Just to be clear, that's still a no on dinner, right?" He ended the call before Charles could cuss him out.

Although he and Gareth were very different, he could appreciate the fact Gareth could laugh through just about anything yet stay focused on the shit that needed to be done. Charles already knew he was the serious one. Then again, he had to be. It wasn't easy keeping all those brothers in check. And right now, he was grateful he had them to keep in line. Otherwise he may have acted unwisely regarding Maxwell. *Now who is going to keep me from fucking up with Rosslyn?*

When she opened the car door and slipped into the passenger seat all thoughts about anything but her vanished. "You smell like flowers."

She smiled. "I was worried I'd smell like the cat."

He had to ask. "First of all, you don't. But why would you smell like the cat?"

Rosslyn wrinkled her nose and said, "I think Miss Snuggles is missing her owners because she follows me everywhere when I'm there. Twice today she showered with me."

"I've never had a pet, but I thought cats hate water."

She laughed. "Would you like to come up and tell her that? I tried, but she insisted on joining me anyway. I even shut the door, but she climbed up on the sink and leaped over the top of the glass door. I wasn't sure who was more scared, me thinking this was some horror movie turning to reality or her with me screaming as though I was being murdered."

Charles could picture the sight all too clearly. Chuckling, he teased, "You're not selling me on getting a pet either."

"Well, you're more the dog type anyway. I can see you walking a Pomeranian Spitz." She pulled out her cell phone then turned it to him.

"What the hell is that? A snowball?"

"No. She's adorable. A white ball of fur. You could take her to work with you because they are great with people. And they also love kids. They only weigh three to seven pounds, so you could take her everywhere with you."

He cocked a brow. "You are joking, right?"

"What don't you like about her?" Rosslyn asked.

"First, if I have a dog, it needs to be bigger than a sock. Second, I want it to sound like a dog."

"She barks."

He shook his head. "Correction, she yips. You know . . . a bark." Charles couldn't believe it but he let a bark rumble from deep within him. "Like that."

"And what would she sound like?" Rosslyn asked.

Oh no you don't. "Sorry, sweetheart. My voice doesn't go that high. But good try."

Rosslyn smiled. "For the record, you definitely sounded part bloodhound and part bullmastiff."

He couldn't hold back and burst out laughing. "Good to know just in case I come across either and need to converse with them."

"I wouldn't advise that," Rosslyn said seriously.

"Why is that?" Charles asked.

"What if you say the wrong thing, offend them, and get bitten? No. It could be a disaster unless you practice first. Maybe you should try again," she teased.

"I can see you're in a playful mood. I guess getting out of work early agrees with you."

She let out a heavy sigh and melted against the seat. "I thought I'd die if I had to stay there one more minute."

Not that he wanted to talk shop, but he did care how her day went. "Rough?"

"Staying awake, yes. I never knew how boring working in an office could be."

That didn't sound right either. Maxwell probably had more business than he could handle. So why not utilize Rosslyn? Even if she wasn't familiar with the process, she was very smart and surely would pick up quickly. *Probably quicker than I suspect. Lawson Steel could use someone like her.* That wasn't going to happen because he wanted, no needed, her more. He needed a reason to look forward to the workday ending. And for him, five o'clock couldn't roll around fast enough.

Even though he was the boss and could come and go as he pleased, he managed through example, not by being the exception to the rules. It made it a lot easier when he needed to address policy issues. *No one was above them.*

But Maxwell didn't work like that. Although Charles knew there was no way Maxwell was really on vacation, he also wasn't known for leaving the company unsupervised that long. He liked to have his thumb on everyone. Maxwell intimidated employees through fear. But Rosslyn, as sweet as she was, didn't seem to be afraid of him.

"I'm glad you're well rested. Maybe tonight we can stay out past nine," he teased. They had called it an early night last night, mostly so things didn't become awkward again. If he hadn't taken her home after their ice cream, she might not have made it home at all.

Rosslyn said, "If we don't ever pull away from the curb, we won't have to worry about what time to get me home."

Charles hadn't noticed they were still parked. She had a way of distracting him just enough that the rest of the world faded into the background.

"I did promise you pizza," Charles said as he pulled into traffic.

"Thin crust pizza," she reminded him.

"You have no idea what you're missing. But thin crust it is."

When they pulled up, the pizza parlor was packed. "Okay, this is when I see why you like take out. We could be done eating instead of standing here waiting for a table."

Charles agreed. He called the hostess over and gave her their orders. He had been tempted to call the owner over and move up to the top of the waiting list. That would've backfired on him. With Rosslyn already calling out the difference in their financial standings, he didn't want to enhance that.

So they would wait, but the take out order cut it to twenty minutes instead of an hour. A small compromise, but one nonetheless.

"If I had planned better, I'd have called ahead with a reservation," Charles said.

"I don't mind waiting. Where do you want to go to eat?"

My house. "We could go to the park."

"Or maybe your house?"

Had he heard correctly or was it just what he'd hoped she'd say. "Are you sure?"

Rosslyn nodded. "My calf is still sore, and I thought maybe that offer to soak in your Jacuzzi might still be valid."

What is taking this pizza so fucking long? His appetite just increased, but it wasn't for anything the restaurant served.

"You should've told me you were still hurting. I can have them deliver the pizza if you want." *Because I'm okay with going to my apartment right now.*

She smiled and said, "Trust me, I'm not that sore. Besides, I'm not going anywhere without that pizza. It smells delicious."

Not half as good as you. "Are you free tomorrow night?"

She tilted her head up at him. "We haven't finished our date tonight."

"I know, but since you promised to give me one week. I'm hoping we can see each other every night."

"You're not afraid you're going to get tired of seeing my face every day?" Rosslyn asked.

He was more afraid of how much he was going to enjoy it. "No. But I'm not doing all the work here. I planned the last two dates. It's up to you tomorrow night."

Her eyes got wide. "I planned last weekend. That should be enough to give me a pass on doing any more planning for a while. Besides, this is your city, not mine."

"Okay, then you can make the plans this weekend since you were so creative last weekend."

She sighed. "Charles, I know I just saw my parents, but I was hoping to go and see them again this weekend."

"Sounds good." She hadn't actually invited him, so he was inviting himself. "You think Brandy has the room vacant again?"

Rosslyn blushed. "I'm not sure she would want us back."

"There's only one way to find out."

"Can we leave early Saturday?"

"Of course. I know you want to spend more time with them." He hated the fact her mother wasn't doing well, so he would make sure to get there as often as she wanted to go.

"I do, but I was thinking we could do something different too."

He wasn't going to try to guess what she considered different. "What would that be?"

"Magnet fishing."

"I've done some deep sea fishing. Caught a three hundred pound tuna once. Not sure if I've heard of a magnet fish."

She snickered. "It's not a fish."

"I thought you said fishing," Charles said.

"I did. Magnet fishing. You use a rope and a magnet."

Charles shook his head. "Forgive me for living in the city too long, but I never caught a fish with a magnet. Usually use a hook and bait."

"We're not out to catch fish."

"You've got me. What is it we're after then?" Charles had no idea what she was talking about.

"There's so much junk in the bottom of rivers and lakes that I spend my time doing something good for the environment and try to see what metal I can pull up from the bottom. You should see some of the stuff I've dragged in. One time I even snagged a shopping cart."

He laughed. "You amaze me. I think you should plan all the dates."

"Wait. What? Why?"

He smiled and said, "Because you come up with the most original ideas."

She stepped closer to him and whispered, "Your ideas aren't so bad either. Now could you do me a favor?"

"Anything, sweetheart. What is it?"

"Put a rush on that pizza so we can get out of here," she said softly.

He looked down at her and knew it wasn't because her feet were tired or her leg sore. Charles winked. "We'll be out of here in five. I promise."

He would've walked out and said screw the pizza, but he wasn't a teenager who couldn't control his needs. But damn, it wasn't easy. God, he missed holding her. And knowing what lay ahead of them only made it harder. Literally.

12

Each night they were together had been better than the one before. He'd hated driving her back to her apartment. Once he was lying naked with her, he didn't want to let her go. At one point he'd been so comfortable he almost offered to bring Miss Snuggles there so there would be no excuse for her to leave.

Those words never left his mouth but had shocked the hell out of him even contemplating saying them. They hadn't made it through the entire week and he was already thinking of ways for this to continue. How was it possible one look into those eyes of hers was all it took?

He knew she was up because she'd already sent him a good morning text. It was Friday and Charles hadn't made a plan for tonight's date. Sadly he couldn't come up with anything as unique as hers. There was no way he was that boring, was he?

Charles could come up with a million things to do. Hell, he'd even thought about flying her away for a night for a romantic dinner on the beach. But he didn't want to wave his wallet around because that would only make her run. He needed to come up with something equally romantic but something anyone could do.

Taking her back to his place for another night of love making definitely was on the top of his list, but he wasn't going to win her heart with mind-blowing sex. Well, at least not with that alone.

Impressing someone like Rosslyn wasn't easy. So far the closest he'd come was the concert in the park and the fireworks. Everyone knew Friday night was a big date night. But it was raining so outdoor stuff was out, and he didn't want to go to a museum. Dancing would be an option but he wasn't into the club scene and had a feeling neither was she. He wasn't opposed to finding someplace intimate, laid back.

Charles knew exactly who to call.

"Twice in a week. Before you know it, we'll actually make time to hang out again," Sal joked.

"Why don't we pull the guys together for a poker night?" Charles suggested.

Sal laughed. "That would be great, but it seems you and I are the only bachelors left. Mike is on kid number four and Ronnie just had twins."

"Twins? God, I hope they aren't anything like him or his wife is in for trouble," Charles half joked.

"It's worse than that. They are girls. But I have a feeling you called for something else. Is it Grayson?" Sal asked.

Oddly enough, the only time he didn't think about Maxwell was when he was thinking about or with Rosslyn. "No. I wanted to know if your friend still plays in a jazz band."

"I saw him last weekend. Why?"

"Can you find out where they're playing tonight and reserve me the best table?"

Sal sighed. "I thought you were going to chill out a bit so

I don't have to hear it from my mother. Seems you have a short memory."

Charles knew it would get back to Sal's mother. That part of town talked. "Don't worry, we're not going to her place for dinner, which won't make her happy at all."

"Now we're talking. Give me a few minutes and I'll text you the information. Table for two, correct?"

"Yes. And for tonight."

"Got it the first time you said it. Now why don't you do some work and let me plan your date for you," Sal teased then hung up.

He normally spent a hell of a lot more hours in the office, first one in and last one out. Since that hadn't been the plan this week, he better kick his ass in gear and concentrate.

As he reviewed the latest proposals, he was impressed. This was one of the best deals he'd seen in a while. At first he thought it was Ethan as it had his flare. But the name on the bottom wasn't his. It was Dylan. He picked it up and looked closer. There was no way this was Dylan's, at least not Dylan's alone.

He leaned back in his chair and smiled. Finally they were pulling together. Sadly it took Charles being such a hard-ass to accomplish it. As long as they all stood together, even if against him, it was progress. A year ago not one of them would side with another.

Charles called the one person he could share this with.

"Hi Dad, how are things?" Charles wanted to make sure his father was in the right frame of mind. The last few years, although there didn't appear to be any good reason, his father seemed to slip into periods of depression. It was hard for Charles to understand, because he'd never experienced that himself. But he could empathize with those who did suffer from it.

"I'm good, son. I heard you've met someone. Are you calling to deliver some good news?"

"Not that kind, Dad. But yes, I'm seeing someone. We're taking things slow." That wasn't exactly true. Seeing each other every night and sleeping together wasn't what his father would consider slow. But times had changed. People didn't get married right out of college, and there was no need to have children before the age of thirty. Hell, he was pushing forty and not even thinking marriage. Commitment of some kind, well . . . that was a different story.

"That's good to hear. I have to admit, I was surprised."

Not as much as I was. "I didn't call to talk about her."

"Oh. Do you need my help?"

His father was still adjusting to being retired, even though it had been a few years. Charles knew it would be hard for him to relinquish the reins entirely. Eventually he'd have to. And this new development was a step in the right direction.

"Seems the brothers are beginning to work together."

"You mean on the business or aligning themselves against you?" his father asked.

"A little of both. Which in my book is a good thing."

"It is. So do you think it is time for you to present the contract to them?"

He wanted to, but doing it before dropping the bomb on Maxwell was dangerous. Maxwell had a way of obtaining information and this was one piece he couldn't risk. It would mean Lawson Steel wouldn't be a privately owned company any longer. Being the seventh generation at the helm, he wasn't ready or willing to dissolve this tradition. Not without a fight.

"No Dad. I need more time. But it will be soon. I have something else I need to take care of first."

"Does it have to do with your young lady?"

In a very roundabout way, yes. But no way in what his father was thinking. "She will be affected."

"Charles, I'm glad to see you are not focused strictly on work."

"Dad, you lived and breathed work."

His father laughed. "And yet I still got married, had six children, and enjoyed my family time. Unless you forget about those days."

He hadn't. It just seemed so long ago. And as Charles got older, he'd tried to escape the family and hang out with Sal. Being at home with all his brothers had been a reminder of the responsibility that would, one day, be passed down to him. *And here it is.*

"Don't worry, Dad. I'm not out to follow in your footsteps. Six boys are crazy."

"Your mother would disagree with you. I'm not sure I would." He laughed. "Why don't you bring your friend down for a visit? I'm sure your mother would love to meet her."

"We're not at that point yet, Dad." That sounded weird because he was going to see her parents again this weekend. Was he intentionally keeping her away from them? There was a good reason, but she was bound to question that, and he needed a good explanation ready for when she did.

"Don't wait too long. You're not getting any younger."

Most people had to hear these things from their mothers. But Charles knew why his father was bringing it up. *No Dad. I'm not going to have a son just to make you happy.* "Dad, I have another call coming in. I'll keep you updated."

"Good. And bring her down."

"Sure, Dad. I'll call you soon." He ended the call before he was asked how soon was soon. The older his father grew, the more persistent he became. Charles was beginning to worry there might be something going on with his father that he hadn't shared with anyone yet. *God, I hope there isn't something wrong.*

Seeing Rosslyn's mother, who was younger than his parents, made him think more about the future. Rosslyn's mother was maybe fifty-five years old. That didn't seem all that old anymore. He always knew not everyone saw retirement age and lived their golden years doing what they didn't have time for when they were young.

It made his father's words hit home. Working himself to death wasn't something he feared, but not stopping to enjoy life now played on his mind. He wasn't sure if he could give Rosslyn all the credit, but she definitely played into the equation. He was turning thirty-nine in a few weeks and at the top of his game. No one could ask for more. Yet looking closer at his life, for the first time he wanted more, and it had nothing to do with business.

Charles wasn't out to catch up to his friends Mike and Ronnie. But there was a piece of him that envied their lives. Neither was rolling in cash, yet each of them was happy.

Was Rosslyn the roadmap he needed to achieve such bliss? He wasn't sure, but he was definitely willing to explore that option.

A few minutes later he received a text from Sal. Perfect. This was one date she wouldn't forget. *Hope she likes jazz.*

Rosslyn had been surprised when Charles told her what they were doing. She had never actually seen a live jazz band before. They had a table so close you could actually see them playing each note.

"This is so nice."

"I'm glad you're enjoying it," Charles said.

I enjoy anything we do together. But she didn't want to

scare him off. Things really were amazing between them. In her mind, there was no way this was ending next week. It was only getting better. And tomorrow they were back in her hometown with the room at the B&B already booked. The difference was this time her parents knew they were coming.

"Are you two enjoying the show?" one of the band members asked as he approached their table.

"You guys are amazing," Rosslyn said.

"Thank you. But I was told this young man you're with can play as well. What do you say? Want to play your girl a song?"

Oh my God. This was the most romantic thing anyone had ever done. When she turned to Charles to tell him, the look on his face said it hadn't been part of the plan. Before she could tell him it was okay, he didn't need to, another man approached.

"Of course Charlie wants to play."

"Sal, what the fu—hell, are you doing here?" Charles snapped.

"I figured if I'm ever going to meet the sweet thing my mother keeps talking about, I was going to have to make it happen myself." He extended a hand. "I'm Sal, and you're the beautiful Rosslyn."

"Sal—"

"I know. Hands off." Sal winked at her. "He's lucky he saw you first."

Rosslyn blushed and giggled. This was the first time she'd met any of his friends. And as soon as Sal called him Charlie, she knew they would get along just fine. "Would you like to sit with me while *Charlie* plays?" she asked.

Charles shot her a look of surprise, then leaned over and whispered teasingly, "Traitor."

She smiled and asked, "You're really going to do it?"

He gave her a kiss on the top of her head as he got up. "Like you two left me any choice."

Rosslyn clapped as she watched Charles take a seat and accept the saxophone he was handed. He wiped off the mouth piece and gave it a few test blows. Soon the room erupted in the sweetest sounds she'd ever heard. She wasn't sure he was the best, but each note was played for her.

As the melody continued, she noticed Charles was transforming right in front of her eyes. He became relaxed and the music flowed from him into her.

Sal leaned over to her and said softly, "I can't believe he's really doing it."

"Why?"

"I don't think he's played in about fifteen years. His father told him he was wasting his time. There were greater things for him in life, meaning working himself to death. Sadly, playing the sax was something he used to enjoy."

"Looks like he still does." She could tell by his body language. "Are you an architect too?"

Sal shook his head. "No. I'm a police officer. None of Charlie's friends are in his field. Mike drives a garbage truck and Ronnie is a plumber."

Charles hadn't mentioned any of them. If it wasn't for Mama, she wouldn't know about Sal either. She wasn't sure Sal intruding on their date was what Charles wanted, but she was glad he had. It gave her a bit more insight Charles hadn't told her about. *He's doing what he thinks he has to. Not necessarily what he wants to.*

They were not that different. She was doing the same thing for her parents, just not to the extent he was.

The song was over and the crowd cheered. She stood up and clapped the loudest. Charles handed the saxophone to another member of the band and walked over to the table.

"God, that was wonderful," Rosslyn said.

Sal laughed as he shook Charles's hand. "Only someone in love would think that was anything other than horrendous."

Rosslyn wrapped her arms around his neck and said, "I could listen to you play all night."

He pulled her closer. "There are a lot of things I want to do tonight, but none of them include the sax."

He claimed her lips and the crowd once again roared their approval. Public displays weren't her thing, but she couldn't bring herself to pull away either. The promise of yet another sweet night in his arms was stronger than any embarrassment she might feel.

Sal's voice was the one interruption they couldn't ignore. "I'm not sure about you guys, but I think the band is waiting to play again. You two are blocking everyone's view."

Charles pulled back but didn't release her. "Want to stay or go?"

Although she didn't want to let him go, she wanted this time out with him too. And if she was lucky, she might learn a bit more from Sal.

"Maybe listen to a few more songs before we go?"

He held the chair for her and once she was seated he turned to Sal. "This is a table for *two*."

Sal called over the waitress who was already bringing another chair. "You should know by now, I think of everything."

Charles gave him a warning look and then turned to her. "Would you like to stop for some dessert after? I'm sure Mama would love to hear how our evening went."

Sal got up from the chair and said, "That's low."

Charles laughed. "Guess you *didn't* think of everything now did you?"

Sal reached out and took Rosslyn's hand in his, then bent

and placed a kiss on it. "It was a pleasure meeting you, Rosslyn. Take care of this one. He needs watching."

She didn't know what to say. Charles ran one of the largest steel businesses in the world. He didn't need her. Surely Sal knew that. "Nice meeting you too, Sal."

As they sat back down and were once again alone, a chill ran through her. She'd been on cloud nine all week. It was perfect. But Sal's words haunted her. He didn't say Charles needed her, but he needed watching. What exactly did that mean? Was there something she didn't know? *Of course there is. We've only known each other for two weeks.*

Everything was moving so fast. And they were going back to see her parents tomorrow. Should she cancel until she knew him better? It wasn't what she wanted to do. And her parents were already expecting him. Her father had invited them to dinner, a real sit-down-at-the-table meal. That was something they hadn't done in more than a year.

For all her concerns about what might be wrong with Charles, she smiled, thinking of all the things that were so right. Nope. She wasn't giving up this weekend. It was something she needed. Charles might need it too. But even more importantly, her parents needed it most.

Charles tightened his hold on her. "You okay?"

She nodded. "I was thinking we could leave after this song."

He smiled down at her. "You must've read my mind."

She leaned back in the chair with her head resting on his shoulder. Rosslyn needed to hold on to the good moments. She knew it could all change in a blink of an eye, and this would be all they had.

13

"I can't believe she actually talked you into magnet fishing. I used to take her when she was a little girl because her mother was afraid she'd get hurt using a hook. But she enjoyed herself so much I could never talk her into real fishing after that." Her father laughed and said, "Which was good too, because she is squeamish. I can't picture her ever taking a fish off the hook."

She shook her head. "Never happening. But I wasn't about to put bait on the line either."

"This is all valuable information to have," Charles said.

"Why?" she asked.

"Because when we are back in Boston, I will know what not to plan."

She laughed. "I can't see us doing a lot of fishing in the city."

Her mother had been in the other room and let out a scream. Her father knocked over his chair, rushing to see what had happened. When she arrived in the living room, he was kneeling by the wheelchair. Her mother was uttering over and over, "Max. Max. Max."

Rosslyn looked at the television and the news was on, but they were talking about the weather. She walked over and shut it off. Her father was trying to calm her, but she continued saying it. Rosslyn knew it was getting late and her mother's mind was slipping. It was best they leave before Charles saw just how bad it could get.

"Dad, we're going to head out so you can get Mom to bed."

"Why don't you help him, and I'll do the dishes while I wait," Charles offered.

She turned and expected to see he was joking, but he wasn't. "Are you sure?"

He nodded. "It's not like I don't do them at home."

Rosslyn wanted to tell him a coffee cup wasn't really considered doing dishes. "Thank you." She kissed him on the cheek and then followed her father into the back of the house.

Her mother's bedroom was on the main floor so there was easy access to everything she needed. Her father slept on the couch. It wasn't the life either of them had expected, but life rarely was.

Her mother was extra agitated tonight, and no matter what they said, she wouldn't stop saying Max. It was hard because there was no rhyme or reason to what triggered her episode. "Dad, I don't mind staying the night and giving you a break. That's what I'm here for, you know."

"No. You go with Charles. It's my . . . honor to be here for her."

Rosslyn's eyes wheeled up. "Oh Dad. She always said you were her prince."

He laughed. "Nope. I'm still a frog, she just had to keep kissing me until I looked like a prince."

She knew her father wasn't going to leave her mother's side until she was fast asleep. *No Dad. It's the princes of this world who need to be more like you.* "We'll see you tomorrow. I'll bring some of Brandy's homemade scones."

"Sweet pea, I want you to take tomorrow off. You worked all week; just enjoy yourself."

"But Dad I'm—"

"This isn't up for discussion. I like him. He seems to be a good man, and if I'm right, you're fond of him as well."

"I am." She was falling for him faster than she wanted, but it was out of her control.

"Then tomorrow make it all about the two of you. No work. No worrying about us. Just enjoy the time you have together."

"Okay Dad." She could promise him anything, but she'd always worry about them. That's what you do when you love someone. Leaving the room she headed back to the kitchen. She thought for sure she'd see the dishes still piled high. Instead they were washed and stacked neatly, waiting to be put away.

"Is everything all set with your mother?" he asked.

"For now. Dad's going to stay with her. I can't believe you did all this. I'm impressed."

Charles laughed. "I hope this isn't the only thing that's impressed you so far."

Teasingly she said, "You did score a large piece of a car bumper today in the lake. That was impressive too."

He grabbed her and pulled her into his arms. "I'm sure I can think of something to . . . impress you with tonight."

Rosslyn blushed and said, "Then let's get out of here."

When they arrived back at the B&B, they barely made it to their room before their clothes were practically ripped off.

Rosslyn leaned in and kissed him hungrily. She needed him like oxygen itself. It was raw passion like she'd never had before. This was a different kind of joining, one at a level of heat that was beyond her control.

Charles picked her up, and she wrapped her legs around him. He growled as her softness pressed against his rock hard abs. He kissed her neck, her shoulder, and her neck one more time before claiming her lips again. His tongue teased her until she trembled with desire. Charles held her tightly as he carried her to the bed.

He placed her in the center before he lay down beside her. She could feel his erect cock pressed against her thigh. She wanted to feel him inside of her. Her body had been on fire with anticipation from the moment they entered the room.

"Charles, I need to feel you inside me," she pleaded.

"You will, but first I need to taste every inch of you," Charles said, his voice husky with need.

Propping himself up on one elbow, his other hand slowly explored her body. Fingers were followed by his lips and tongue. She reached for him, trying to pull him on top of her, but he ignored her as she quivered helplessly. She was being held captive by the sweetest torture she could imagine. He nibbled and licked down her chest to her navel, finally coming to rest on her inner thighs. She opened to him, to take her in his mouth, but he refused. He was making it clear he was in charge. As he continued to kiss her thighs, his fingers found their way to her wet folds.

She ached for more and said again, "Please Charles, I need you now."

His response was to circle her clit with his thumb. Arching her back, she gripped the sheets with both hands and cried out. Charles brought her to the brink of climax and held her there, refusing her flood gates to open.

"Please," she panted. "Please, I need . . ."

He kissed her once again on her thigh. She groaned. This

time Charles did not disappoint her. His thumb was replaced by his tantalizing tongue, and she opened wider for him. Each lick and suck brought her closer. His tongue darted in and out of her. He sucked her clit harder, until the waves of climax rocked through her and she screamed his name again and again. The waves seemed endless. It was a pleasure she had not known before, more intense than she'd thought was humanly possible.

Charles left her for a moment then quickly returned after sheathing himself. He knelt between her legs, lifting them so her knees now rested over his shoulders.

"Now Charles," she demanded.

With his hands on her hips he entered her with one deep thrust.

Oh God. Yes. A low growl emerged from somewhere at the back of her throat. He began to move, lifting her to him again. The pleasure was almost unbearable as he held her hips and drove deeper and deeper inside her, as though he couldn't hold himself back. The sound of his flesh smacking against hers filled the room. The headboard banged against the wall and she swore the windows rattled. She didn't give a fuck. All she wanted was more.

Charles answered her request with faster, harder strokes. She felt her body tense. Her body tingled, seeming as if every cell burst as her climax rushed through her veins. Charles gripped her thighs tightly, plunging deeply, as he exploded within her, bringing her to yet another explosive climax.

Charles collapsed on top of her. His weight while he was still inside her was glorious. They were breathing heavily as he nestled himself close to her.

She wanted to tell him how amazing that was, but no words were going to express the true magnitude of what they just shared. Entwined like this, they gently stroked and caressed each other until they eventually drifted off to sleep.

Charles wasn't going to answer his phone. It was the weekend and, damn it, he was going to enjoy himself. Whatever the issue was, he'd deal with it on Monday.

"You know you can answer your phone. I don't mind," Rosslyn said as they drove back to the city.

"But I do. My brothers are used to always having me right there. It's time they learn to figure shit out on their own. The company won't crumble without me for a few hours." And if it did, then they didn't belong there.

"I shut mine off too. But mostly because I didn't want to hear whatever Brandy was going to say. I can't believe how loud you were last night," Rosslyn said.

Charles laughed. "Me? I think that was *you* screaming my name."

"And who made the bed sound like a freight train coming through the entire house. God, I hope we didn't break the bed."

"If we did, I'll buy her a new one. We might need it for the next time anyway."

Rosslyn shook her head. "I can't show my face there again. I'm sure the entire town is going to be talking about me. Why didn't you tell me the windows were open?"

Charles reached over and grabbed hold of her hand. "First of all, I only opened the window once you were asleep. Second, if they are talking, it's because their lives are boring as hell. And third—"

"Okay, you're right. Who cares what anyone thinks? Well, maybe my dad, but that would be *your* problem, not mine."

He wasn't thinking of her father at the time. But it potentially could become awkward. What was the worst thing that could happen? He probably would ask Charles what his intentions were. Charles would answer honestly. *I care very much about her.* For now, that's all he could commit to. But he believed this was turning into something so much more.

"Are you planning on visiting your parents again next weekend?" Charles asked.

"No. I'm trying to go every other weekend. Why?"

"I was thinking we might want to take a little trip. Someplace where no one knows either of us and you can scream all you want."

She pulled her hand away from his and slapped his playfully. "Stop reminding me!"

"So what do you think? I'll even plan it." Hopefully taking that pressure off her would help seal the deal.

"Charles, you know I can't. I've got the cat to watch for another week." She let out a heavy sigh and continued. "And I really should spend some time looking for what I'm doing next."

"Are you leaving Grayson?" That would be awesome news are far as he was concerned.

"No. My apartment and cat babysitting job will be over, so I need to find another one."

He hadn't thought about that. There was plenty of room at his penthouse, but asking her to live with him was a huge step. What if it didn't work out? He could never ask her to leave without another place to go to. He could always pay for an apartment for her. That way when they needed space, they each had their own.

"Why don't you let me help?"

"Sure. Maybe that's what we can do tomorrow night," Rosslyn said, smiling. "Thanks."

He was surprised she was in agreement. Charles thought for sure he'd need to do some convincing "It's my pleasure. While we look we can grab a bite to eat."

"Okay, but Mr. Grayson is supposed to be back tomorrow. I'm not sure what time I'll be getting off work."

"Should we add looking for another job at the same time?" Charles half joked.

"I hope not. But you never know. He's so unpredictable. I guess if he fires me, I go back home."

"You wouldn't stay in the city?" *With me?*

"Who would hire me here if I get fired from Grayson Corp?"

If people knew Maxwell like he did, they'd only hire people he didn't want. "I'm sure I could help you with that as well."

"I'm not going to work for you, Charles," she said firmly.

"Good. Because I'm not going to hire you. I have strict policies that would make working around you . . . extremely uncomfortable."

"Oh, you mean we couldn't sleep together?" Rosslyn asked.

"No dating at all."

"Boy, you're a tough boss. Mr. Grayson doesn't care about that. As long as you do your job and kiss his ass." She laughed. "For the record, I don't kiss anyone's ass."

He was glad to hear it. "I didn't think you did. But you're right, I'm nothing like him."

"I'm glad. He's not always the nicest person."

"Has he said or done anything to you he shouldn't?" If he had, Charles was going to fucking kill the bastard.

"No. I'm pretty much non-existent as far as he's concerned."

"That might be a good thing." He didn't want her too close with Maxwell.

"In some ways yes. In others . . . not so much. But it is what it is," Rosslyn said.

It wasn't long before they were back in the city and he was pulling up in front of her building. "Do you want me to wait while you take care of the cat? You can stay at my house tonight."

Rosslyn leaned over and kissed him briefly. "This girl needs to get some sleep tonight or I'm going to be dragging my butt into work tomorrow. I might not like my job, but I need it."

When she got out of the car and closed the door, he wished she'd have said yes. She hadn't made it in the building and he missed her already. That was absolutely ridiculous and only confirmed why they shouldn't live together. He liked his space. And right now, he was going home to enjoy it.

As he pulled away he finally turned his cell phone back on. There were at least twenty missed calls from his brothers. He wasn't sure which to call first. So he decided to go the path of least resistance and call Seth. He was the one who rarely had any issues. If he did, he didn't bring them to Charles.

"Hey Seth, what's going on?"

"We were hacked," Seth announced.

"What do you mean hacked?" Charles asked, now wishing he'd answered earlier.

"I mean some asshole was able to get through our firewall and access some of our files. Not everything, because our security team noticed it early. But shit Charles, who the fuck did you piss off to start messing with us?"

His first thought would be Maxwell, but what would he

benefit by getting into their computer files? Maxwell would probably do what he had done to their father and go after his building reputation. That was a lot harder to recover from than some damn missing files.

"No one that I'm aware of. Have you talked to Gareth about it?"

Seth said, "You're the CEO."

"And Gareth has connections," Charles said flatly.

"We all met about this a few hours earlier, you know when we were calling and you were ignoring."

He didn't feel guilty in the least. It seemed as though they'd handled it appropriately. To Charles, that was a positive thing. Once again, they were working together. *Maybe it's been me holding them back from that all along.* Had his need for controlling everything been what had driven them away from Lawson Steel in the first place?

"Seems like I wasn't needed after all," Charles stated.

"No. Gareth stepped in and confirmed that nothing serious had taken place. But this isn't like you Charles. Normally you stand at the helm, and we'd only hear about a problem in a meeting later."

It was him holding them back. Damn it. All this time he'd thought he was leading, just like his father had done to him years ago, but maybe that's not what they wanted, or needed. Should he consider stepping down? Was he not the right person for the job?

As though the universe knew he needed an answer, Seth added, "We're used to you always handling everything. Guess we took for granted that you always would be. This was a good wakeup call that we need to step it up and get more involved."

"I'd like that. I really would like all of your opinions on some ideas." This was a good week to present them too. And when that was out of the way, he could inform them of what he'd been distracted with, besides the lovely Rosslyn. Hopefully they would be as understanding as Gareth and Dylan had been. If they weren't, well, that wasn't going to stop him. This decision wasn't being made as the CEO of Lawson Steel. This was personal. *I'm doing this for Dad.*

After he got off the phone with Seth, Charles returned Gareth's call.

"You're late."

Charles ignored it. "Seth already updated me. I don't think it's Maxwell, but do you think it's linked to the Hendersons?"

"Hendersons? I thought you said that was a dead end?"

"It is. Gia was just playing around. She likes researching old things, but has no real credentials."

"And that's why you mentioned the Hendersons?" Gareth asked.

"Just grasping at straws. I have no idea who would hack into our system."

"Me."

Charles had to be hearing things. Did Gareth just admit he was the hacker? "What are you talking about? You have access to everything already."

"I do. And if you recall, you asked me to make sure everything was good to go for when you dropped the dime on Maxwell."

"And you found flaws that need fixing. Good. Can you fix them?"

"Already done. But while I was in there, I figured I'd pretend to be Maxwell. He'd bypass all the small shit and go directly into your personal files. You would never believe what I stumbled across accidently."

"You were in my personal files? Why?"

"For security reasons. But you're not playing along. Would you like to guess or not?"

He was too tired for games or any kind. "Gareth, I have no idea what you're up to, but you should stop."

"No can do. This is too much fun. Besides, I think you need my help and don't know it."

Charles did need Gareth. *To keep an eye on Maxwell. Not dig into my personal shit.* He wasn't in the mood for starting an argument with him. But he would address it later. "With what exactly?"

Gareth said, "Pulling the family together. And if you haven't figured it out by now, I found the contract. The one Dad created. I have no idea what the hell he was thinking putting that kind of pressure on you. We're all grown-ass adults."

Oh shit. Add that to the files on Maxwell and he just realized his computer wasn't as secure as he'd thought. "He needed me to prove to him I was right for the job."

"That's fucking crazy. We all know you are. No one has the background you do."

"That doesn't change a thing. Unless I get everyone to agree to sign that contract, I'll need to step down and Lawson Steel will—"

"It won't. Have faith. We might not always agree, but when it comes to this company, it is a family business. Owned and run by Lawsons for over two hundred years. We're not changing that now."

He could hear the frustration in Gareth's voice. Charles had felt the same way. "I can't explain why Dad did this, but unless I get it signed—"

"Which you will. Just call a meeting and tell them everything," Gareth blurted.

"You didn't read the entire thing did you? I'm not allowed

to inform any of you of the stipulations. Hell, with you knowing, it means I should step down."

"The hell you are. And for the record, I read every word. It states clearly that you are not to tell any of us. At no point did it say anything about one of your brothers hacking in and coming across the document."

"You can't say anything to any of them," Charles warned. He knew if their father caught wind of it, that would be the end.

"Charles, you are, and probably always will be, the rule follower. There's nothing wrong with that. Hell, it's what we want our CEO to be. But we live life a bit differently. Maybe that's because we weren't stuck being dragged around with Dad all over the place. Mom let us have some freedom. Sometimes too much. But it taught us to take a risk every once in a while. Sometimes it paid off, and other times, well let's just say we're lucky no one ever got caught."

"And what does any of this have to do with Dad?" He already knew his brothers had raised hell when they were young.

"Dad never caught on. He was always so focused on the business that he never noticed the shit we were doing."

"This is not the same at all."

Gareth laughed. "It is exactly like that. Now you call the meeting and let the dice roll."

"You're fucking crazy if you think I'm going to put Lawson Steel on the line like that."

"Charles, trust your brothers."

That's all he needed to say. Simple words, but very effective. "I'll schedule it for the morning."

"Good. Now tell me again why your phone was off. Could it have anything to do with Rosslyn Clark?"

"It may. And once again, still none of your business. By

the way, that type of information is not stored on any computer."

Gareth grunted. "With all the shit I do for you, you won't even let me meet her."

"That's because I like her and she's sweet. And sweet women don't do well around you."

"What does that mean?" Gareth questioned.

"They fall for your pickup lines too easily."

Gareth laughed. "Oh. I see. You're worried she won't be able to resist my charm and I'll steal your girl. Thanks for the compliment."

Charles rolled his eyes. *Whatever you want to believe.* "If you don't mind, I have a meeting to schedule and you must have a conquest waiting for you somewhere."

"That I do. See you in the morning. And Charles, don't lose any sleep over this. It's nothing, trust me."

Famous last words. He ended the call as he approached his building. Going up without having Rosslyn by his side sucked. Even though she never spent the entire night, she was there for most of it.

Tomorrow after work they'd talk, he'd set her up in an apartment and they could start the next phase of whatever this was between them. He wasn't ready to label it, but he knew he didn't want it to change.

14

"Are you serious? Dad really had this drawn up?" Jordan asked.

Charles nodded. "He did and it's binding."

"Does Mom know about this?" Dylan asked.

"I'm guessing not. Dad kept her out of the loop for pretty much anything business related," Charles replied. "He didn't want her to stress about things." *Like raising six boys wasn't enough stress.*

"I can't believe this. I don't know about anyone else, but if you have the contract ready, I'll sign it," Seth stated. "You have always put Lawson Steel first. This only proves, once again, you're meant to be the CEO."

"Agreed," Ethan added. "Just sucks Dad put you in this situation."

"Dad's been trying to put a wedge between us our entire childhood," Dylan said. "It seems now that he's getting older, he's trying to change."

"He tried Dylan, but he didn't succeed. We're all sitting in this conference room right now," Gareth said. "And I second Seth's suggestion. Let's sign it and let it be done."

Charles looked across to Dylan. He was filled with anger. Was it because he felt forced to follow his brothers? That's not what Charles wanted. If they didn't sign willingly, then they shouldn't sign at all.

He didn't want to single any one of them out. That would cause another problem all together. "I don't want anyone to feel as though they need to sign this. Dad wanted me to earn this on my own. There are no hard feelings if you don't think I have."

Gareth was the one who turned to Dylan. Dylan said, "Don't look at me; that was years ago. I had my reasons for not wanting Charles to succeed. He was an arrogant ass. Or maybe I was. Okay, we both were, but that was over a long time ago. I don't agree with what Dad did, but if it meant that we all had to sit down and talk this out, I'm glad he did it. I can't remember the last time we all sat at a table together."

"When Dad retired," Jordan stated.

"And before that?" Seth asked.

Charles answered, "One holiday, I'm not even sure which one. Mom dragged us all home for dinner."

"She was shocked when we all showed," Gareth said. "Damn it. We all have our own lives, but this isn't right."

"No, it isn't. But right now I'm not in the mood to see Dad. I'd probably tell him how wrong he was," Jordan said.

"He didn't mean any harm. His upbringing wasn't like anything we've experienced. Dad didn't come from a loving family. It was all based on one thing, making money. I'm not even sure if our grandfather knew anything else," Charles told them.

"I can't remember him," Dylan said.

"Count yourself as lucky. For all the things Dad is not, we need to appreciate him for what he is. He did everything because he loves us. Even now with this contract, it was because he loves us all. Dad never had a favorite and this was his way of showing us that. Granted, I'd like to think there were options, but we all know he wasn't that guy." That's why Maxwell was able to set him up all those years ago. Dad thought one way and never veered from it. Charles swore not to be that way. Listening to his brothers talk about him now, he wasn't so sure he'd achieved that.

Dylan waved to Seth to slide the contract over to him. He pulled out a pen and signed on the dotted line. Then he held it up. "Who's next?"

Gareth took it then Seth. Jordon followed suit. When it came to rest in front of Ethan he shook his head.

"I meant it, Ethan. You don't need to sign it," Charles said. That's when he realized he wasn't like his father. He could see the bigger picture and wasn't pulling the strings on any of them.

Ethan turned to Charles and asked, "Before I sign this, I want to make sure this is the only thing you've been hiding from us."

Charles glanced over to Gareth, then Dylan. It was time. Actually it was overdue. "There is something I want to discuss."

"Dad?" Seth asked.

"Lawson Steel?" Jordan asked.

Dylan added, "Maxwell Grayson?"

Charles said, "All of the above. Hope no one had any place to be, because this is going to take a while."

He opened his briefcase and pulled out the file on Maxwell. He knew this family tension actually started long before Maxwell Grayson. It went back to their grandfather and his abuse of their father. That wasn't his story to tell. If anything it would only make them question their family history even more. So he decided to stay focused on what was necessary. *Bringing Maxwell down.*

They spent the next four hours reviewing every single document both he and Gareth had compiled. He intentionally didn't mention Gareth's part in any of this. But when it came down to what Maxwell had done to Lawson Steel years ago, the room fell silent.

When they started talking again, Seth asked, "Are you doing this for Dad, Lawson Steel, or yourself?"

"In the beginning I wanted to avenge what he'd taken from Dad. But then I discovered this wasn't just about Dad or Lawson Steel. Maxwell had crushed companies that weren't as resilient as ours. With each new development, I knew I had to stop him. Confronting him wasn't the way to do it. I wanted justice. That's when I decided to go to the Feds."

"What are you waiting for?" Ethan asked.

"I wanted to talk to you all first. This doesn't just affect me. If for some reason that asshole gets off, he'll come for me, for us. We need to make sure this is what we all want to do."

"Like we have a choice. It's only a matter of time before he comes for us again," Dylan said. "I'm not sitting back and waiting. You have my vote."

"Mine as well," Seth added.

Jordan and Gareth agreed, and that once again left Ethan. He looked around the room. "I'm not sure I want to be asked to any more meetings." He pulled out a pen, signed the contract, and slid it over to Charles. "Congratulations, Charles. It's official. You're the permanent CEO."

"Thank you," he replied.

Ethan added, "You also have my approval to go after that bastard."

"Gareth, you have a few connections at the Bureau. Do

you think you can get this in the right hands?" *One that Maxwell can't touch.*

"You've got it. It'll be taken care of tonight."

"Great." It was done. All of it. Charles was mentally wiped out. "You guys want to call it a day and grab a bite to eat?" They nodded. "Great. I know this place outside of the city. It's not fancy, but the food is fabulous."

He'd never taken any of them to Mama's. Until that day, he'd kept his two lives separate. But as with Rosslyn, it was becoming impossible. Charles and Charlie were merging. How much so was left to be seen.

On the way to eat, he sent a quick text to Rosslyn, HOW IS YOUR DAY?

She replied, BORING. THE BOSS DIDN'T SHOW.

That meant she was heading out on time; unfortunately he'd just promised his brothers a great meal.

PICK YOU UP AT SEVEN. That gave him plenty of time and she could take care of the darn cat.

SEE YOU THEN.

I hope everything goes as smoothly tonight.

Rosslyn had brought her laptop with her, but she didn't know why. Searching for a place to live could be done on her smart phone. But she figured it'd be a lot easier sitting together. Now on the couch, she realized the computer wasn't the issue, it was being so close to Charles.

But there was something different about him tonight. He seemed so much more at ease. "Did you have a good day at work?"

He smiled. "One of the best in a long time."

"That's great. It's nice starting the week off right," Rosslyn replied. "I just have no idea why Mr. Grayson didn't come into the office. He was scheduled to. There were meetings scheduled all day, which I needed to move around."

Charles cocked a brow. "He didn't call you to let you know?"

"No. And from what I hear, he didn't call anyone. It's so strange. He's not even picking up his cell phone." Was it her imagination or did his lips curl slightly? She knew he wasn't a fan of Uncle Max, but happy that he hadn't been heard from was a bit too much. "You don't seem too concerned."

"Should I be?" Charles asked.

"I guess not. I'm not even sure why I am. For all I know he's done this before. But no one really talks to me there. The only one who did got fired." *I miss you, Liz.*

"If you're worried, why don't you call your friend? Maybe she knows something."

"That's a good idea. I'll do it tomorrow if he doesn't show up again." She leaned over and rested her head on his shoulder. "In the meantime, you promised me you'd help me look for a place. I tried while I was at work, but had no luck."

"Do you care where it is?" Charles asked.

"Just someplace safe." Not that anyplace was totally safe, but there were areas with a high crime rate that she wanted to avoid.

"That's simple. I'll make a call and you can move in anytime you're ready."

She lifted her head and said, "What do you mean move in? You're supposed to help me find another apartment that needs babysitting, with our without the pets."

"When did I say that?"

"Last night. You offered to help me with an apartment." She got it. He misunderstood and thought she wanted help finding one to rent. "Sorry. I should've been clearer. I can't afford anything in the city. Not if I'm going to continue to help my parents. So I need a place where I can stay for free."

Charles shook his head. "I said I'd help you with an apartment. If you'd rather pick it yourself, that's fine. I'll take care of the rest."

She looked at him puzzled. "Are you offering to pay for my apartment?"

He nodded. "You can't. I can. Very simple."

She stood up and paced the room. Her blood was boiling. *What kind of girl does he think I am?* Walking around some more, she huffed then stopped. Facing him again she said, "You know I can't pay you back, right?" He nodded again. That infuriated her and she paced again. *Bullshit. That's what this is.* Accepting an apartment was going to be like being paid for . . . sex.

He might not have intended to, but he just made what they shared feel cheap. Walking over to her laptop, she closed it and said, "If you don't mind, I'd like to go home now."

Charles got up and asked, "Rosslyn, what's the matter?"

"I can't believe you need to ask." Why didn't he see anything wrong with what he'd said? Maybe he was so damn rich that money could be easily thrown around. *Like Uncle Max does for his so called lady friends.* Being around Liz, Rosslyn learned some very unappealing things about that side of her family. She was disgusted. If Charles was suggesting the same thing for her, he could kiss her Alexandria Bay ass. They might look all sweet and quiet up there, but they weren't pushovers. *And not for sale either.*

"Rosslyn, I didn't mean to upset you. Why don't you sit down and we'll talk this out?"

What she wanted was to back the conversation up about ten minutes and hit delete. But there was no backing out of this. No matter what he said, she'd feel the same way.

Every time he bought her dinner or any gift, she'd associate it with this. Even if he hadn't meant it the way it sounded, her heart was hurt. *If I stay, I'm setting myself up for more. And I can't keep up with him.* Eventually she'd feel indebted to him and that was a bad place to be for any relationship.

"Charles, maybe tomorrow, but not tonight. I need to think right now."

"Please, Rosslyn, don't leave. Not like this," Charles pleaded.

Everything within her wanted to let it go. But was that the right thing to do? *No.* Looking him square in the eyes, she said, "Charles, you asked me to give you one week. Today is exactly that. But we're from different worlds. I can't live in yours and you can't live in mine. I think it's best that we just say goodbye."

It felt like a knife was digging into her heart, and she was the one planting it there. She didn't need to call it off. She could go home and think about it. Maybe tomorrow it wouldn't seem so bad. Yet Rosslyn let her emotions gain control and that was never a good thing.

Charles put his hands on her biceps and said, "You can't be serious. This past week has been amazing. Actually so was the week before that. Don't throw it away because I said something stupid."

Tears rolled down her cheeks from both frustration and heartache. "Charles, I didn't come to New York City to meet someone. I came to work. This is all too—"

"This is something unexpected, but it is still something good. Please, Rosslyn. I know you're angry, but promise me you'll sleep on it, and we can talk about it tomorrow."

Her eyes stung and she didn't know what to do. Twenty-four hours wasn't going to change anything. But at least she could regain her composure. Nodding, she said, "I'll call you tomorrow." She pulled away and started for the door.

He was right beside her. "I know you're angry, but I'm not letting you go home alone. It's late. Don't waste your breath arguing. I'd never forgive myself if anything happened to you."

She followed him down to the car and the ride home was in silence, mostly because she couldn't bring herself to talk. Doing so might cause the waterworks to start. When they pulled up to her building she said, "Thank you."

He reached out and held her hand. "Rosslyn, I know it might not seem like it, but I care very much about you. I'd like to pick you up tomorrow so we can talk, in person. Would that be okay?"

She was glad he wasn't telling her but was asking her instead. Nodding she said, "Seven. But we don't go to your house. Maybe coffee instead." If he wasn't going to agree to that, then he wasn't seeing her.

"I'll be here. Sweet dreams."

Not likely. She left the car and headed to the apartment. As she opened the door, she felt drained. She hadn't been back here so early in an entire week. The only one happy right now was Miss Snuggles who wouldn't leave her alone.

Rosslyn stripped off the dress she'd worn for Charles and went into the bedroom. All she wanted to do was close her eyes and sleep. Odds were that was going to come after a lot more tears. Thankfully they wouldn't go on forever.

15

Rosslyn didn't want to go into the office, but she did. She couldn't believe what was awaiting her. The place was crawling with law enforcement. They asked her for her ID and asked how long she'd been working for Grayson Corp. She never told them they were related, but then again, they didn't ask.

When she sat down at her desk, she realized Uncle Max's door was open. Was he here? She went in only to find someone from the FBI inside.

"Can I help you?" she asked.

"You are?"

"Rosslyn Clark. I'm his . . . secretary/assistant."

The man walked over to her and asked, "When was the last time you spoke to Mr. Grayson?"

"Friday I think. Why?" The man didn't answer her.

"What did he say when he called?"

"Not much. He let me go home early because it was slow without him here."

"You didn't find it odd that he didn't return?"

She shrugged. "I haven't been employed long enough to know his habits yet. Is he in trouble?"

"Why would you ask that?"

Duh. "Because you're with the FBI. You're in his office, and I highly doubt he gave you permission to be here."

"I asked why you think he might be in *trouble.*"

That was easy to answer. The guy was shady. But he was her boss and, more importantly, her uncle. She wasn't going to speak ill of him. Well, if she was sworn in at a court of law she would, but that was it.

"Like I said, I haven't been here long enough to make any assessment of Mr. Grayson, including his character." That at least was more of a fib than a lie. Not that there was a difference, but fib sounded so much better. "If there is nothing else, I'd like to get back to my desk."

"We'll be in contact if we have any more questions."

Rosslyn went to her desk and resisted the urge to call her father. When she came to work for Uncle Max, she knew it would be interesting, but this was more than she'd bargained for. Sitting with nothing to do made her uncomfortable. It wasn't as though she could call Max and ask if she could leave. She debated asking the FBI if she needed to linger.

As she pondered that question, she realized she hadn't received her daily text from Charles. They had been like clockwork. He always wished her a good morning and then firmed up plans for that evening. Maybe he decided not to meet her after all. She had been harsh, probably more than she needed to be. After sleeping on it, she had every intention of apologizing. Of course, that was only if he was still speaking to her.

The way her morning started, who knew if she'd get to see Charles, even if he did reach out. She might be taken in for questioning. But with knowing nothing, she had no fear of being in trouble for doing something wrong. The most Max had allowed her to do was make coffee and schedule appointments.

Her nerves were getting the best of her and wreaking havoc with her system. She got up and started down the hallway. The agent called out, "Where are you going?"

Rosslyn turned to him and said, "The ladies' room."

"We'd like to speak to you."

"Now or can it wait two minutes?"

"Now. Come with me please." She stood there and he added, "You have a choice. You can come with me willingly or in cuffs."

Some days it didn't pay to get out of bed. Rosslyn walked toward him into Max's office. He walked around the desk and sat in Max's seat. She stood until he pointed to the chair. Once seated she waited. *Speak only when spoken to and you can't get in trouble.* Of course she wasn't sure if she already was.

The man just leaned back and stared at her. She had already told him all she knew, which was nothing. She wiggled and wished they had allowed her to use the ladies' room. At the rate conversation wasn't taking place, it might be a long day. That was okay, she got paid by the day. Or at least that was what it was supposed to be. Who knew what was happening now.

When he spoke he asked, "Are you involved with anyone, Miss Clark?"

That wasn't a question she was prepared for. "I don't see how that is any of your business."

"If I'm asking the question, it is my business. Now answer it. Are you involved with anyone?"

Since she had broken it off with Charles last night, she could honestly say no. They were meeting for coffee; that

185

was it. Nothing further than that was going to happen. "I am not."

"Are you sure about that? Because lying to me would not be wise. And you, young lady, are acting like you are hiding something."

"My odd behavior is because you refused to allow me to use the ladies' room," Rosslyn said, holding firm to her answer. If Uncle Max found out she'd been sleeping with Charles, he'd flip. God knows what he'd do. The agent reached into the desk and pulled out the large envelope she had placed in there on Friday. "You can't go through his things without a warrant."

She didn't know that for sure, but that's what they said in the movies. He ignored her and said, "I find your lack of cooperation disturbing." He opened it, pulled out photos, and laid them out on the desk. Her jaw dropped. It was her with Charles. They weren't just talking either. One picture even had his hand on her breast. It seemed to have been taken through a window while she was at his penthouse.

Was Uncle Max watching her? Why?

"I can explain these."

"You don't need to. They tell a very interesting story. What I don't know is why are you sleeping with Maxwell Grayson's main competition?"

Because I have fallen in love with him and can't stop myself. That was the truth. One that she wasn't about to admit to the agent or anyone else. Not even to Charles. That was the final straw that said they didn't belong together.

"I didn't know who he was at the beginning, but it is over now."

"Really? Why is it I don't believe you? If I went to Lawson Steel and spoke to Mr. Lawson, would he say the same thing?"

God I hope so. "I cannot speak for him. But I ended it last night."

"Why?"

"Once again, that is none of your business."

"This is part of an investigation. And if I deem it important, I won't stop until I have the answer."

She was a horrendous liar. And somehow she had the feeling the truth would come out anyway. "He wanted to pay for an apartment for me and I refused."

"And you stopped seeing him over that?"

"Yes. It made me feel . . . well it wasn't nice." Her feelings definitely weren't important to him. She wasn't sure if they still were to Charles.

"And that was the end of it. Just like that?"

"If you mean did I cry myself to sleep and regret ever meeting him? Then the answer is yes. Now if you don't mind, I'm going to pee myself if you don't let me go now."

"One more question. Did you know Mr. Grayson was tracking you?"

Shaking her head, she said, "I don't know why he would. I normally live a very simple life."

"That's not how I'd describe these pictures, but then again, my idea of simple might not be the same as yours. You may go now. I'll be in contact if I have any questions."

She practically ran down the hall. Not so much because she needed to pee, but she was sick to her stomach, seeing the photos of her and Charles. Some were quite intimate. *How could you, Uncle Max? How could you?*

Seth entered his office and asked, "Have you seen the news?"

Charles had intentionally kept the TV off. Nothing going to distract him from talking Rosslyn into forgiving him.

And maybe giving it another week. He hadn't slept a wink last night and his head was pounding. "No. Why?"

"That Feds are at Grayson Corp. I heard they are talking to all the employees too."

Rosslyn. Sorry sweetheart, I would've warned you but . . . who was he kidding? He wasn't going to tell her. Not as long as she worked for Maxwell. "That's no surprise. Gareth delivered the file yesterday. I have to admit they acted faster than I thought, but then again, we had some serious documentation in there."

"I don't think that's why they are there. There's a rumor that Maxwell's private jet might have crashed."

What the hell? "You're not fucking with me, are you?"

In a serious tone Seth said, "I'm not Gareth."

"Shit. I can't believe this." His mind was racing. Timing of this really couldn't be worse. "You said rumor. But they're not sure are they?"

Seth said, "So far the news said the jet was last seen on radar a few days ago. Since they did not show for their dinner engagement yesterday, they assumed something must have happened."

Charles wouldn't put it past Maxwell to do all this for the media blitz. "Don't believe everything you hear. Until they find the jet and have a positive ID, I'm not buying it." It was more likely he figured out what Charles was up to, and this was his way of avoiding the Feds. He couldn't mention that to Seth, because he didn't want to instill panic in the family for no reason. If it looked like the two were connected, he'd update them.

"I know you don't like the guy, but damn, you sound kind of cold."

"No. I'm just not going to feed into the media frenzy until I know there is a reason to. Besides, we're talking about

Maxwell Grayson. You don't think he'd pull a stunt like this? You read the file yesterday."

"He is one fucked-up individual so nothing is off limits. But as a company we need to prepare ourselves. I'm sure his clients are going to feel that way. They are already in a panic. Some have called us to know if we can fill their orders if, in fact, Maxwell's dead."

"Wow. And you thought I was cold. But that's business. There is no time to stop some of these major projects. There's billions of dollars on the line. Maxwell's clients aren't going to sit back and mourn his loss, not if it means they are losing money. Because in the long run, we know why he got their business in the first place."

"Undercut the competition. Undercut us."

"Exactly. And now they are panicking. Desperate." *And we'll be happy to take their business too.* Charles would like to think Lawson Steel was prepared to meet the demand. He'd confirm personally that was the case. Charles never wanted to make a commitment to a client which he couldn't deliver on. There was so much prep time, and everything needed to be coordinated months in advance; they couldn't ask a client to wait. If it was true, and Maxwell was gone, that was a game changer and not just for Lawson Steel.

"Seth, I need you to make sure any of Grayson Corp clients are treated with kid gloves. They are probably testing the waters to see if we would take them on. But if Maxwell is alive and shows up tomorrow, they might drop us once again."

"I've got it. And I'm going to see what Gareth can find out too. Maybe one of his connections can find out what really is going on."

"Good. Hey, I've got to go. Can we talk about this tomorrow?" Charles needed to check on Rosslyn. If she had heard the news, she might be panicking about her job. Of course he might be the last person she wanted to see, but he had to try.

"Tomorrow? With everything I just told you, you're okay with stepping out?"

He could see the concern on Seth's face. "I need to check on Rosslyn. She works for Maxwell. She might know more than we do." It provided an acceptable answer, which wasn't a lie.

"Someone on the inside. That's a change. Okay. We'll talk tomorrow."

As soon as Seth was out of his office, he tried calling Rosslyn. It went directly to voicemail. So he dialed Grayson Corp and that also went to voicemail. If she was in the office, she probably didn't want to answer in case it was the media.

There had to be so much going through her head right now. Rosslyn already was concerned about money. Maxwell signed her paycheck after all.

He could always drive there, but that would cause questions if the media snapped his picture there. He chose not to leave her a message. *If she needs me, she knows she can call me.*

The problem was, he wanted her to need him. Not that he hoped she had issues, but he wanted to be the one she turned to. If he didn't hear from her today, he'd go to the apartment building at seven as planned. He hoped she would be there and happy to see him.

Charles needed to get out of there. He opted to take a drive. Between Rosslyn not speaking to him and Maxwell pulling this shit, his day was fucked. He needed answers about both of them. Oddly enough, what was going on with Rosslyn mattered a lot more to him.

I don't care if I have to drive all the way to her parents' house, I'm going to talk to her again. This isn't over. He'd spent the last few years fighting for revenge, now he was going to fight for love.

He'd never said that word to a woman. It was the only explanation for how he felt. It was all happening too fast, and that was why he'd screwed up last night and tried paying for an apartment for her. Charles replayed it over and over in his head. She had every right to be pissed at him. The fact that she stood her ground only made him love her more. She was a proud, strong woman. He should've known and respected that. And when he saw her next, he was going to make sure she knew it.

16

She knew she should have picked up the call from Charles, but after seeing the photos of them together, she couldn't speak to him. The media had been all over the place, and she didn't want to give them anything else to talk about. When she found out the FBI wasn't there because they thought Max had done something illegal, but believed he might be dead, she knew she needed to be with her parents.

Even though they weren't close to Max and Laura, they were still family. Someone had to mourn their loss if in fact they were gone. Goodness knows that none of the employees were going to. *They were only going to miss the paycheck.*

She felt bad because part of her felt the same way. It was scary thinking of how you would feed your family, provide a roof over their heads, and keep them safe when the source of doing that was ripped out from under you.

She would like to think Max had made provisions for his employees, but he barely cared about their lives before, why would he think about what would happen to them after he was dead? Yet even with all his faults, and they were numerous, she still hoped the media was wrong.

The bus pulled into the station and she got out. She went around the back and grabbed her suitcase. This wasn't going to be an overnight stay. If Max was gone, there was no reason to be in the city any longer. And since Miss Snuggles's owners came home early, she didn't have a place to stay either. It seemed the timing of everything was aligned in a way she couldn't have planned. Right down to saying goodbye to Charles last night, even before she knew it was destined to end.

Being back home wasn't going to be easy. Although she hadn't been gone long, it was the weekends she'd returned that were going to haunt her. She had joked with Charles, saying she couldn't return because the people in town would all be talking. The truth was, being there was going to be salt in her wound.

Would telling her parents about Max be easier with Charles by her side? Of course. She could've leaned on him for emotional strength. Would it also bring a new level of issues without him? Yes again. She was going to be hounded with questions she really wasn't ready to answer.

That was the problem with bringing someone home to meet the family. Her dad thought Charles was a nice guy. She couldn't tell him what happened, but she needed to say something. Walking home from the bus station gave her plenty of time to think about it.

Did she have to tell her parents she broke it off? Not right away. If they asked, she could truthfully say Charles worked during the week. After a few days, she could tell them dating long distance wasn't for her, and she had decided to focus on herself and her future right now. *That might actually work.*

It was close to being true, except for the fact it wasn't. Rosslyn was in love with Charles. She even forgave him for his stupid suggestion. But after the FBI called her back in for questioning, she wasn't sure she knew Charles at all. The FBI never said he was a suspect in her uncle's disappearance, but their line of questioning suggested it. *Has he ever talked to you about Mr. Grayson? Did he ever make any threats toward him? Did you know he was investigating Mr. Grayson?*

Rosslyn had known they were rivals, but never suspected at this level. Charles had gone to the FBI on her uncle. What on earth would make him do such a thing? And even worse, not tell her anything about it. And the pictures of her and Charles together weren't because of her. Her uncle was watching Charles, and she just happened to be caught in the middle of two adversaries out to take each other down.

She had to hear all about it from some agent who only wanted to see her reaction to that news. And he got it too, because she had run over to the trash can, vomited, and almost passed out. It was as though everything had been pulled out from beneath her, every ounce of joy and happiness within her crushed in only twenty-four hours.

The truth of why she was home was simple. She was hiding. Her emotions were all over the place. She had wanted to storm to Charles's place and demand he explain himself. Then again, she didn't want to ever see him again. But that thought only caused her to cry more. She really did love him. The only thing she could do was run. The only place she could go was home.

At least she could deliver the news in person to her parents. It could've been done on the phone easily. Sadly, any tears for Uncle Max or Aunt Laura were because of how they had wasted their lives. They had all the money and power, but they never did one damn good thing with it. If they were gone, what would they be remembered for? Nothing of any true value, unless your name on a building was what you sought in life. Yes, she was sad, sad that some people loved money more than anything else. And if they weren't dead, she highly doubted either of them would change.

But Charles didn't seem like that at all. He had truly seemed to enjoy his visit with her parents. Max never would've stepped foot in their house, never mind wash the dishes. If it hadn't been for her seeing his car and apartment, Rosslyn never would've known Charles was as wealthy as Uncle Max. He didn't flaunt it. Even their dates, whether planned by her or him, were what ordinary people would do. *Why couldn't he be as poor as me?* That would've changed everything, and they would probably still be together. But that wasn't the case, and she highly doubted Charles was going to walk away from all his money just to prove he loved her.

She shook her head. He never said he loved her. Then again, she hadn't told him either. With everything that was going on, she thought for sure he'd have tried harder to reach her again. One missed call surely wasn't all the effort he was willing to put in. If he did love her, he'd have rushed right over to be with her. Then again, with all the FBI agents around, he might have been trying to avoid them. *Nope. I don't care. If he loves me, he'd have come.*

Her phone rang and she pulled it out of her pocket. *Damn it.* Once again it was another unknown number. She shut it off. How did the media get access to her personal phone number? They could call all they wanted. She wasn't talking to any of them. All they got was her voice mail.

She turned the bend and saw her house. The truck parked in the driveway, which wasn't surprising. Her parents were always home. She walked up the path and dropped her suitcase on the porch. She'd take it inside later and unpack. Right now she just wanted a huge hug, no questions asked. Rosslyn knew one of the two was guaranteed.

Opening the door she called out, "Mom. Dad." There was

no answer, so she went into the kitchen, but no one was there. That was odd. She searched the entire house, but her parents weren't home. That made no sense. The truck was there.

Her heart skipped a beat. Something must've happened to her mother. If an ambulance had taken her, surely Dad would've ridden with them. As she pulled out her phone, she heard a vehicle pull into the driveway. She rushed to the porch and was speechless. She knew that car all too well. *What the hell is he doing here?*

Rosslyn wanted to tell him to go back to the city; she didn't want to see him. That was the furthest from the truth. She wanted to see him, hold him, and ask a hell of a lot of questions. But before she could say anything, the passenger doors opened. He wasn't alone.

Mom? Dad? She rushed down the stairs and over to them. "Where have you been? I was worried something might have happened."

"Charles showed up a few hours ago, and after all the talking we did about the old days, he offered to take us for a drive so he could see some of those places."

She looked at Charles who wasn't saying a word. *You will by the time I'm done with you.* Turning back to her father she said, "Let me help you get Mom inside."

"Don't worry, Charles will bring her."

Charles walked around the car and scooped her mother into his arms. "I've got you, Mrs. Clark." Her mother giggled as he carried her inside and placed her in the wheelchair.

She took hold of her father's sleeve and pulled him out onto the porch. "Dad, what's going on?"

"I guess I should be asking you that. Your young man showed up here looking for you. If it weren't for the fact we'd seen the news early, we'd have been worried. But once we knew about Uncle Max, we knew you were coming home."

"I wanted to tell you in person."

Her father shook his head. "I might be getting old, sweet pea, but I'm not that old. I can recognize a lovers' quarrel when I see one."

"Dad we're not—"

"Hush. Don't waste words on me. You should take him for a ride and talk to him. Tell him how you're feeling."

"Dad, you have no idea who he is. He's . . . Charles Lawson. Lawson Steel."

"Yup. I know."

"He told you?" she asked.

He shook his head. "I recognized him the first time you brought him home. His face is all over those business magazines."

"You read those things?" Now she was really puzzled.

"We get them because your mother liked to follow what Uncle Max was up to."

She had seen them plenty of times, but they were always by the fireplace. She figured her father had picked them up to burn.

"Does Mom know about Uncle Max?"

"Her mind is slipping a lot. I didn't tell her. It wouldn't matter. In a few minutes she'd forget anyway. It's better we don't mention it."

She wrapped her arms around her father and said, "I'm sorry, Dad. I wish there was something I could do to make this all better."

"You can. Go talk to that man of yours and listen to what he has to say."

"But Dad, we are from two different worlds."

Her father laughed. "You think I can't relate? Look at me

197

and your mother. But we made it work. You can too. That is if you want to. Only you know the answer. And you can't make it work until you talk to him."

"But Dad, this isn't the time. Uncle Max is missing."

"No, sweet pea. They found the plane and there were no survivors. Uncle Max and Aunt Laura are gone, along with the pilot."

She shook her head. "I want to feel something, but . . . but . . ."

"Rosslyn, he was my brother-in-law; I know exactly what you mean. The times we did see each other weren't very pleasant. But he was still our family."

"I feel horrible that I just up and left like that." There was a lot more to it, but she wasn't sharing that.

"There was nothing there for you. Well, except for Charles, who is patiently waiting for you while entertaining your mother. Now go before he changes his mind."

She hugged her father and said, "I love you, Dad."

"Love you too, sweet pea."

Rosslyn went inside and saw Charles sitting beside her mother's wheelchair. He was talking to her about when they went magnet fishing. The sight of them really touched her heart. *He is a good man. Just a very rich one.*

Walking over, she gave her mother a quick hug and said, "Mom, I'm going out for a drive with Charles. We'll be back later, okay?"

"Yes. You know your curfew. Be home by eight."

Rosslyn smiled. "Yes, Mom." She waved for Charles to follow her outside. Her father slipped past them and into the house.

They got into the car and Charles asked, "Where do you want to go?"

"How about our fishing place? It's private there and we can talk."

Charles nodded and started the car. As they drove he said, "I'm sorry about your uncle and aunt."

He knows. "Thank you."

"Why didn't you tell me you were related?"

"It's by blood only. We were nothing to him." *Other than an embarrassment.* "I actually feel bad for all the other employees. I have no idea what will happen to Grayson Corp now."

"I'm sure they will find jobs. And probably with someone who appreciates them." He turned to her and said, "I'm sorry. I shouldn't have said that about him."

"That's okay. I don't want you holding anything back. Actually I don't want to either. I'm sorry I said what I did the other night. I was hurt and . . . confused. I was going to call you and let you know, and then all this went down."

"I was a jerk. I said that because I was too afraid to say what I wanted to."

"And what was that?" she asked.

"I wanted to ask you to live with me. But I kept telling myself it was too fast. We needed time. We needed space. The truth was, I was scared."

"Scared? Of what?" He didn't strike her as someone easily scared of anything.

He pulled into the parking spot and shut off the car. Then he turned to face her. "Of what I was feeling. It felt too good to be true. And I was trying to hold on to it without crushing it."

"You mean me?"

"I mean us. I fell in love with you, Rosslyn, and had no idea how to deal with it. And in trying to keep control, I lost it all. So when you didn't answer your phone, I went to your apartment and found the owners there. I knew where you'd go. So here I am."

That was the very short version, but there was only one thing she cared about at the moment. *He loves me.*

"Charles, can you back up please."

"Sure. To where?"

Smiling she said, "To the part where you said you love me."

He reached over and took her hand in his. "Rosslyn, love doesn't seem to be a strong enough word. It's like you've become a part of me, and when you weren't there, I wasn't whole. Nothing feels right without you. I love you."

Her heart was beating fast and the words echoed in her mind. "Charles, I love you too. That's why I left."

He cocked a brow. "Shouldn't you run to me, not from me?"

"Charles, I need to protect you."

He laughed. "I'm almost twice your size and you want to protect me? From what?"

"The FBI. They are looking into my uncle's disappearance, I mean death. They think you have something to do with it."

"What makes you think that?"

"Because they were questioning me about you. About us. They said you were out to get my uncle."

"Unfortunately, part of that is true. I was out to expose your uncle's crocked business dealings. I have been working with the FBI, gathering information on him. I'm sorry to say, but he wasn't a very nice man."

She already knew that. "And they don't think you had him . . . killed?"

"God, no. And I hope you don't either."

"No. I just . . . well I didn't want to make you look

guilty," she admitted. Somehow she knew she'd be the one throwing him under the bus and purely by accident. "I'm not really good at dealing with their questions."

"You don't have to worry, sweetheart. I'm not a suspect. And actually my sources say that it was a lightning strike that may have taken out the jet. They don't know for sure, but that's their first thought."

"Good. I guess. I mean, that no one killed them. But they're still gone either way."

"Yes. Your father and I had a good talk while waiting for you. He explained the family dynamics to me."

"You know what my mother did?" She was surprised because they never told anyone. No one in Alexandria Bay even had a clue they were related to a billionaire. *Or that my Mom once was one of them.*

"He did. He told me everything."

"What a love story."

"Do you know what he said?" She shook her head. "That your mother never missed the money because she had everything she ever wanted—you and your dad."

"And we have her. I just don't know for how much longer." Her heart broke thinking about it.

Charles said softly, "What I've learned since I met you is that time can be broken down in many ways. But it's who you spend it with, what you do with it, that defines your life. You're right, they are a beautiful love story. And I hope you can see past my faults so we can have one of our own."

Tears rolled down her cheeks. "I thought you said you weren't a romantic. Now you have me bawling like a baby."

He reached up and wiped her tears. "If they are tears because you love me, let them flow, and I'll catch every one of them."

She leaned toward him and put her arms around his neck. "They are, Charlie. And they are all for you."

She winced and pulled back. He looked at her. "Are you okay?"

"Let's just say bucket seats and a stick shift aren't the most comfortable when it comes to making up and making out."

He laughed. "I hear there is this wonderful B&B in town. It gets rave reviews. What do you say we give it a try?"

She laughed as she slipped back into her seat. "I don't know if they have any vacancies."

"I'm sure when Brandy sees us pull up, there will be." He gave her a playful wink.

As they made their way back to town, she let go of all the worries she'd been carrying. Her parents were going to be okay. She would always make sure of that. Her job, well she'd find another. But what she couldn't do without was the person sitting beside her. He had somehow become the glue holding her together. Nothing seemed quite so difficult when she knew they would face it as one.

She leaned over and said, "Is that offer still valid?"

"You might need to clarify that a bit. Which one exactly?"

"To live with you."

She saw his face light up with the biggest grin yet. "I think I might want to move in with you."

Rosslyn laughed. "I'm homeless. I'm going to have to live with my parents. I don't think that would be ideal." Not with the looks they get at the B&B.

"That's not what I meant. I mean buy a house here in Alexandria Bay. You could be close to your parents and I can—"

"No, you're not leaving your job. I can learn to like the city." It was different when her mother left the family. She was disowned. But she didn't want Charles to leave his family and his friends.

"I thought we could commute. Do three days in the city, four up here. What do you say?"

"You're serious, aren't you?"

"If you haven't figured it out, I'm not the jokester in the bunch. So, is that a yes?"

She smiled, leaned over, and kissed his cheek. "That's a yes. I love you, Charlie."

"I love you too, Rosslyn. Now if you don't mind, I'm about to break the speed limit."

Rosslyn placed her hand on his upper thigh teasingly and said, "What are you waiting for? Pedal to the metal." She burst out laughing as the car jolted when he popped the clutch, switching gears in all the excitement. The engine roared as they raced down the roadway. She knew they were about to have some of the best make-up sex the world had ever heard. *Let's make the entire town jealous. I don't care as long as I have you.*

EPILOGUE

"This can't be right. Are you sure?" Rosslyn asked.

"I'm positive. Everything is in order and I have confirmed its authenticity."

She turned to Charles and asked, "Do you know what this means?"

He nodded and grumbled. "You're now my biggest rival."

She slapped his arm playfully. "I'm serious. Everything, Grayson Corp, the money, the property, all of it is mine. I don't understand it." She turned back to the lawyer and asked, "How is this possible when we were disowned."

"There was a stipulation that everything was to be divided between the children of both Carla, your mother, and Maxwell, your uncle. Since he had no children, it all goes to you."

Her hand trembled as she held the papers, still not comprehending the magnitude of what she'd inherited. "I don't know what to say."

The lawyer said, "Nothing. All you need to do is sign here and it is yours. You will have full access to all accounts."

She looked at Charles and asked, "Should I do this? Sign?"

"Why wouldn't you?" he asked.

"Because I don't want to be your rival. If this is going to come between us, I don't want any of it."

He smiled. "Sweetheart, whether you're a billionaire or a pauper, you'll always be my rival, but in the very best way. This is your decision, but remember, you're not your uncle. What you do with this, is up to you."

She looked down at the paper and thought of all the employees who wouldn't lose their jobs. Then of Liz, who she could hire back. And of her parents who wouldn't need to struggle to pay medical bills. That was just the beginning of the list of what she could do. Turning back to him, she said, "But in the business world, I'd be your competition."

"Yes, but in all that matters, you're my world. That trumps business any day. Believe me, we can make this work. But only if you want to. I love and support you in whatever you choose to do."

She reached over, picked up the pen, and signed her name, Rosslyn Clark-Lawson. Then she handed it back to the attorney and said, "I'd like it if you could hold off making any announcements. I would like my husband and I to let our families know first."

"Of course. Please let me know if you need anything at all. I'll have all this processed and logged today. And by the way, I see congratulations is in order."

Rosslyn placed her hand on her well-rounded belly. "Thank you."

"Once again, I'm sorry this has taken so long. We hadn't anticipated a will from your Grandfather to be what superseded your Uncles will. The courts seemed to drag their feet on it as well. A unique situation I'd say."

I wouldn't have excepted anything less. "I'm just glad the company wasn't lost in the process. Hopefully most of the employees will return."

"The Grayson Corp. has been through a lot. I'm sure it will recover from this setback as well."

She and Charles got up from their seats, her with a little help from her husband, and headed out the door. She couldn't believe all the changes that had taken place. Her small little world had grown tremendously, and in a few months, it was expanding again. The doctor had given her a scare, saying it was twins. She was embracing all these changes, but she would never forget the look on her sweet husbands face when the doctor had hinted twins. Yet the initial look of shock quickly became one that she had come to know very well, love. And any fear she might have felt had vanished as well. She knew Charles would be beside her all the way.

Rosslyn turned to Charles and asked, "What am I thinking, taking on a company and all that goes with it? I have enough on my plate already."

He smiled down at her and said, "You were thinking that you have a wonderful loving husband who is going to help you every step of the way."

She laughed, "You said that when I got pregnant too, and look at your flat abs and my stomach."

"Okay, I meant with diapers and feedings. Sorry sweetheart, but this part is all yours. Besides you already know if a man ever had to have a baby, the world would come to an end."

She laughed. "Then it's a good thing I'm here to carry on the Clark-Lawson name. But I'm serious Charles; do you know what we just took on?"

"What I know is there isn't anything we can't do together.

And besides, I have some brothers who would do just about anything for you too."

"How did I get so lucky?" she asked.

"It was simple, you had me the moment I laid eyes on you. And I'm never going to let you go."

"Good. Because I'm not going anywhere without you."

"I love you, Rosslyn."

"I love you too, Charlie." The rest of the world could have Charles. She grinned and knew who he would always be to her. Her playful, kind, and loving Charlie.

The End

Continue with Book 2: The Billionaire's Charade

The Billionaire's Rival

Charles Lawson carries the weight of the entire family's future on his shoulders. As CEO of Lawson Steel it is his responsibility to ensure their legacy continued for the next generation. First on his agenda is to clean up loose ends from the past. Doing so is risky and if he fails, the price could be great. It's a risk he's willing to take.

Rosslyn Clark loves her life as is, but family is everything to her. When her parents find themselves in a crisis, all she loves is at risk. Whether she likes it or not, sometimes change is inevitable.

As Charles prepares to seal the deal, he finds one beautiful blonde stands in his way, and things become complicated. Can he continue with his original plan and look at her as collateral damage or has Rosslyn become something more to him?

Rosslyn finds herself caught between two powerful men, one she works for, the other, his rival. Will she do what is expected of her, or will she walk away from everything and follow her heart?

****

Barrington Billionaires Series:

Book 1: One White Lie (FREE!)

Book 2: Table For Two

Book 3: You & Me Make Three

Book 4: Virgin For The Fourth Time

Book 5: His For Five Nights

Book 5.5: New Beginning Holiday Novella

Book 6: After Six

Book 7: Seven Guilty Pleasures

Book 7.5: At the Sight of Holly

Book 8: Eight Reasons Why

Book 9: Nine Rules of Engagement

One White Lie

Brice Henderson traded everything for power and success. His company was closing a deal that would cement his spot at the top. The last thing he needed was a distraction from the past.

Lena Razzi had spent years trying to forget Brice Henderson. When offered the opportunity of a lifetime, would she take the risk even if the price would be another broken heart?

Do you love reading from this world? Continue with Always Mine from my sister, Ruth Cardello, Her series will mirror my time line. It isn't necessary to read hers to enjoy mine, but it sure will enhance the fun!

****

Betting on You Series:

Book 1: The Billionaire's Secret (FREE!)

Book 2: The Billionaire's Masquerade

Book 3: The Billionaire's Longshot

Book 4: The Billionaire's Jackpot

Book 5: All Bets Off

Book 6: A Rose For The Billionaire

Book 7: The Billionaire's Treat Novella

The Billionaire's Secret

Billionaire Jon Vinchi is a man with one passion: work. His friends decide to shake him up by entering him as a prize at a charity event.

Accountant Lizette Burke is dressed to the nines and covering for her boss at a charity event. She's hoping to land a donor for the struggling non-profit agency that employs her.

She never expected to win a date with a billionaire.

He never thought one night could turn his life upside down.

One lie stands between them and their happily ever after. Too bad it's a big one!

****

Southern Desires Series:

Southern Spice

Derrick Nash knows the pain of loss. But is he seeking justice or revenge? He doesn't care as long as someone pays the price.

It is Casey Collin's duty at FEMA to help those in need when a natural disaster strikes. After a tornado hits Honeywell, she finds there are more problems than just storm damage. Will she follow company procedures or her heart?

Can Derrick move forward without the answers he's been searching for? Can Casey teach him how to trust again? Or will she need to face the fact that not every story has a happy ending?

****

Turchetta's Promise Series:

For Honor

Looking for a new Romantic Intrigue? Then you will love the Turchetta's. You met them in both the Betting On You Series as well as Barrington Billionaires Series. Now it is time for an up close look into their lives.

Rafe Turchetta may have retired from the Air Force, but his life was still dedicated to fighting the injustice of the world. There was one offense that went so wrong, and it will haunt him, as it continues to destroy him on the inside.

Deanna Glenn was being tortured by a tragedy, one that she couldn't share with anyone. Time was running out and she needed the lies to cease before she started to believe them herself.

Healing meant returning to where it all went horribly wrong years ago. For Deanna she needed to take on a new identity. For Rafe, that meant doing whatever he needed to in order to get her to speak the truth.

When danger rears its ugly head will Rafe follow his heart and protect Deanna even if it means never learning the truth? Or will Deanna sacrifice her happiness and expose it all?

****

Books by Ruth Cardello

ruthcardello.com

Books by Danielle Stewart

authordaniellestewart.com

Do you like sweet romance? You might enjoy Lena Lane

www.lenalanenovels.com

BY JEANNETTE WINTERS & LENA LANE

Muse and Mayhem Series

Book 1: The Write Appeal

Book 2: The Write Bride

Book 3: The Write Connection(2019)

Made in United States
North Haven, CT
28 August 2022

23293461R00124